ANSWER MY PRAYER

SID HITE

ANSWER ❧ MY PRAYER

HENRY HOLT AND COMPANY

NEW YORK

Henry Holt and Company, Inc.
Publishers since 1866
115 West 18th Street
New York, New York 10011

Henry Holt is a registered
trademark of Henry Holt and Company, Inc.

Published in Canada by Fitzhenry and Whiteside Ltd.,
195 Allstate Parkway, Markham, Ontario L3R 4T8.

Library of Congress Cataloging-in-Publication Data
Hite, Sid. Answer my prayer / Sid Hite.
        p.   cm.
    Summary: When the angel Ebol comes down to the land
of Korasan to help the forester's sixteen-year-old
daughter, Lydia, he finds himself involved in romance,
political intrigues, and other escapades.
    [1. Fantasy.   2. Angels—Fiction.]   I. Title.
PZ7.H62964An   1994   [Fic]—dc20   94-39235

ISBN 0-8050-3406-4

First Edition—1995

Printed in the United States of America on acid-free paper. ∞
10   9   8   7   6   5   4   3   2   1

Many thanks to my editor,
SIMONE KAPLAN,
for her patience and creative input.

I see a sleeping stranger.
I see a stormy sea.
I see the sovereign sighing.
Behold!
There is a kiss beneath a jeefwood tree.

—THE FORTUNE-TELLER

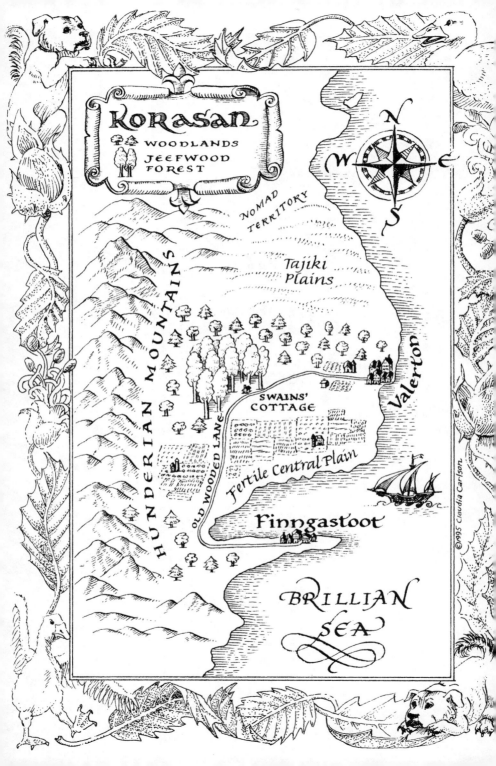

ANSWER MY PRAYER

❧ I

Sixteen-year-old Lydia Swain could hardly contain her excitement as the horse-drawn wagon bumped and creaked along the old wooded lane. The day had finally come. Here she was—on her way to the regent's festival that took place each spring in the seaside village of Valerton. Visions of Saturday night waltzed wildly through her head. For the first time in her life she would be attending the annual Artisan Guild dance.

As the amber hand of twilight began to tickle the treetops, she whispered to herself, "In twenty-four hours I'll be getting dressed and ready to go."

Lydia sat alone in the back of the wagon, huddled under one of her mother's handmade quilts. Up front her father, Lloyd, held the reins loosely and whistled a folk song. He was practicing for the upcoming competition. Glenda Swain, Lydia's mother, rested her head upon Lloyd's strong shoulders and hummed softly.

Mixed with Lydia's excitement was a tinge of apprehension. She had grown up in the remote Jeefwood Forest that her father managed for the Artisan Guild, and as a result there was much she did not know about dances, dresses, or village life.

The Swains had departed from home at noon and spent the rest of the day traveling through the vast woodlands that separated them from the coast. Only in the last hour had they begun to pass by the occasional small farm. Lloyd had promised his wife and daughter that they would arrive in Valerton in time for a late supper with the Bells, the family of Glenda's sister, Ella. Yet after a delay with a wobbly wagon wheel, they were now hoping instead for a snack before bedtime.

The horses were going much too slow to suit Lydia. She was not concerned about supper; she was regretting the hours missed with her cousin, Antoinette Bell. Antoinette was a year younger than Lydia, yet she had spent her life in Valerton, and to Lydia that experience had bestowed an enviable sophistication upon her younger cousin. Lydia could hardly wait to see Antoinette and start asking questions about the dance.

Soon Lydia heard her mother calling, "Sweetheart, stand up and look before the sun sets."

Lydia did as her mother suggested and was promptly rewarded with a distant view of the Brillian Sea. It appeared to extend eastward from the coast in an infinite sheet of shimmering gold. Hugging the shore like an uneven splatter of pewter was the faint outline of Valerton. Lydia held it steadfastly in her sights until dusk prevailed over the vague gray shapes.

She trembled as she sat back down and wrapped the quilt around her shoulders. It was not the chill that had gotten to her; it was the wild waltz of her imagination.

"Another hour," she mumbled expectantly, "and Antoinette will be telling me things to remember."

Although Lydia Swain and Antoinette Bell were bound

4

by blood and immense affection for one another, there was a pronounced physical contrast between them. Lydia was tall, with hair the color of autumn wheat, while her cousin was short, with ink-black tresses. Where Antoinette's eyes were loden green, Lydia's were a clear, baby blue. They did have similar mouths, but their cheeks, chins, noses, and foreheads were cast from radically different molds. Antoinette's face was roundish and soft, making her pretty at a glance, whereas Lydia had sharp, angular features that required a moment's study before revealing their beauty.

The truth was: Lydia did not know whether she was beautiful, or ordinary, or worse. Living deep in the woods as she did, her own attractiveness was a matter she rarely pondered. Glenda and Lloyd had explained to her that beauty existed on the inside, and since that seemed perfectly logical, she had taken them at their word. Yet *rarely ponder* does not mean *never*. Now, as the wagon bumped along the road to Valerton and Lydia projected ahead to the big dance, she fretted about whether she was pretty at all.

There is an old saying that beauty is in the eye of the beholder. It is a true saying, but beauty also lives in the heart of its holder. Indeed, the heart is where beauty thrives best of all. And this being the case, Lydia should not have harbored a single doubt—she should have known she was as pretty as a pretty girl can be.

The first foot of night was stepping onto land when three deer bounded into the lane behind the wagon and stared at Lydia. "Hello," she muttered. In polite reply, the shy creatures dipped their heads before turning and running in the direction from which the Swains had just come. Lydia watched their white tails bob away in the darkness, and as she did her thoughts continued along the old lane . . . until finally she had returned in her mind to the modest cottage she called home. Promptly she began to worry about Walter and Weezie. Walter was her diminutive brown dog, and Weezie was her large long-necked goose. Weezie was a bit of a bully. Even when Lydia was there to referee, the old goose had a penchant for charging after Walter and pecking furiously at his retreating hindquarters.

After a few moments Lydia sighed and decided not to worry. After all, she reminded herself, Walter was wary and quick. He had long ago learned to keep one eye peeled for Weezie and one eye on the lookout for possible escape routes.

Soon Lydia's thoughts turned again to Valerton. Thanks to a natural channel in the sea, the village was the principal port in the small, mostly rural nation of Korasan. The country lay east of the Hunderian Mountains, south of the Tajiki Plains, and west of the Brillian Sea. In the center of the country was a broad plain of rich volcanic soil. Blessed by Korasan's moderate climate, this fertile plain was ideal for the farming of crops. As a result, the economy of this small nation was based primarily upon the production of fruits, grains, nuts, and vegetables. Due to the nearly impassable mountains in the west, the seemingly endless plains in the north, and the unpredictable sea to the east, Korasan has been practically cut off from the rest of the world since it was first settled during the Middle Ages of man. Except for the commercial junker-ships that sail into Valerton each autumn, or the rare appearance of a nomadic trading caravan on the edge of the Tajiki Plains, the country has continued to exist in relative isolation.

Although isolated, the country does not lack culture. In fact, as the world goes, it is a rather civilized place. The family unit is highly honored, the arts are widely respected, and violent crime occurs so infrequently that there are no statistics to measure its rise or fall. It is a land where honest work is still the key to success. As a rule, Korasanians are kind, industrious, and well-mannered.

Of course, there are always some exceptions to the rule.

Should the reader have heard of Korasan before, it is probably because of the jeefwood tree. This giant, slow-growing plant yields a remarkably beautiful, light, and durable wood that is the envy of craftsmen all over the planet. Over ninety percent of the world's known jeefwood forests are found in Korasan, and the nation is quite famous for the fine art and furniture it produces from this quality wood. In fact, this is Korasan's link to the outside world: If not for the country's export of jeefwood products, it is unlikely any junker-ships would risk sailing the treacherous Brillian Sea each autumn.

Lydia did not realize she had fallen asleep until she was awoken by the clopping of hooves on cobblestones. When her eyes blinked open, she was instantly elated by the welcoming lights of Valerton.

She threw off her quilt and stood. Finally—they had

arrived. And oh, just look! There was a broad boulevard on her left where people were sitting in outdoor cafés. Young couples strolled hand in hand through the streets. A man peered into a decorated shop window while the woman at his side admired her reflection in the glass. An elderly fellow tipped his top hat at two old ladies attired in lace-trimmed frocks. An audience of squealing, rosy-cheeked children encircled a dancing monkey. A gang of teenagers clustered idly around a fountain.

Lydia stood slack-jawed in awe. Not only was the village bustling on this eve of the regent's festival, it was dressed for the event. Windows were framed in tinsel . . . chimneys were draped with streamers . . . doorways were adorned with wreaths. It was more than her hungry eyes could absorb.

Suddenly she heard her name. Looking up, she spotted Antoinette leaning from a third-floor window. "Lydia. My dear Lydia."

"Antoinette!"

"Oooh! I was so sure you would never arrive."

"It did seem to take forever."

"Longer than forever," Antoinette countered with a shout. "I've been waiting that long, plus an hour."

"Hello, dear." Glenda Swain smiled upward. "Be careful you don't fall."

"Hi, Aunt Glenda. Hi, Uncle Lloyd. Hold your horses right there. I'm coming down."

"As you say," chuckled Lloyd.

"Nice to see she hasn't changed," Glenda noted with a grin.

Several blocks from where the Swains were being received on the front steps of the Bell residence, a young artist named Aldersan Hale stood alone in a drafty attic, contemplating his latest creation. The attic was located above a seed store that closed each evening at six (the hour when mice opened for business). It had low, slanted ceilings with shingle nails sticking through, floors that creaked, and countless cracks in the walls. A collection of sputtering oil lamps provided the only light. Still, it was an ideal studio for Aldersan. Rent was free, and except for the enterprising mice, it was a place where he could ponder and sculpt in reflective solitude.

From time to time, there are certain individuals who are so naturally skilled at a particular task that people say they were born with a gift. Aldersan Hale was one of these individuals. His gift was a special understanding of wood. Perhaps it was bred in the bone. His mother and father were both guild members, she a furniture designer, he a master builder. Yet their skills were learned, whereas Aldersan's talents were evident from childhood. When he was but a tot of five, he was already astounding friends and neighbors with the detailed figurines he whittled from the odd bits of jeefwood his parents brought home from work. By the age of seven, working only with a pocketknife and his imagination, he was carving birds that appeared ready to fly, horses that seemed ready to run, and realistic little people who looked like they might talk.

By the time Aldersan Hale reached adolescence, it was common knowledge that he had the soul of a great sculptor. At the age of seventeen he had matriculated beyond apprentice status and become a full-fledged member of the guild. And so by day he earned a living carving ornamental motifs into the headboards of Korasan's famed jeefwood beds, while at night he worked as an artist.

On this night before the festival, Aldersan was anguishing over the facial details of the griffin he had been carving since midwinter. Griffins are mythological creatures with the face, wings, and forelegs of an eagle, and the hindquarters and tail of a lion. They are thought to be diligent observers, and are traditionally employed as guards or chaperons. The sculpture was a large work, his first serious commission, and he wanted to be sure he got the expression just right. He knew the torso and the wings were correct, and he was rather proud of the movement he had given to the creature's strong tail, but the eagle face was giving him problems. The regent, Victor Bimm, who had offered Aldersan twenty gold talens to create the sculpture, had been specific about two things: "Have the griffin done in time for the festival, and be certain the thing appears dominant and fierce."

Aldersan—usually so clear and incisive about his art— was nearly undone by the griffin. Perhaps he was befuddled because dominant and fierce were characteristics of which he knew little, but more likely he was at a loss because he had never seen a griffin before. For whatever reason, he was anxious and uncertain about the sculpture, and no matter how long or hard he studied the mythical creature, he could not seem to locate its essential inner spirit.

He worked into the wee hours—sanding a feather here, filing a talon there—looking for the soul of the griffin. And as he worked, the village slept. Or rather, most of the village slept, the exceptions being Antoinette Bell and Lydia Swain. They lay side by side in Antoinette's top-floor bedroom, keeping whispered company with the night.

For many hours Antoinette attempted to tell Lydia what it felt like to kiss a boy on the lips. It was not an easy thing to describe. Regardless of what she said, some element seemed to be missing. (Much of her difficulty in expressing herself stemmed from the fact that she had kissed only one boy on the lips, once, very briefly, and only because they were standing in the dark and she had missed his cheek.) Still, she reached deep into her vocabulary and tried to convey the mystery of what she had felt.

Lydia was a patient listener. She did not care if Antoinette drew her words from the whole cloth of memory or the checkered fabric of her imagination. It was the feeling that interested the two cousins, not the anatomical details.

Eventually Antoinette began to wind down. "Oh, I guess you had to be there," she yawned, then added speculatively, "Who knows? Maybe tomorrow night you will find out for yourself."

"Who, me?" Lydia was startled by the concept.

"Sure," Antoinette whispered. "You might be dancing along with some boy, and then something might come over him . . . and . . . well, he might just try to kiss you."

A sudden inexplicable fear surged through Lydia. She could hardly fathom the prospect of dancing with a boy, much less the notion that one might try to kiss her. "An-toinette, please," she gushed. "There is a very good chance that no one will even ask me to dance."

Antoinette yawned again and rolled onto her side. "Someone will, I'm sure."

"Like who?"

"I don't know who. Just someone. Night."

"Night," Lydia replied in kind. For the next several hours she lay with her eyes open, listening to the loud pounding of her heart, waiting for the big day to dawn.

⇥2

Early the next morning, as the inhabitants of Valer-ton were rising to greet the day, a thick blanket of nimbostratus clouds dimmed the skies over the village. For several hours it appeared as if showers were immi-nent, but a few moments before the official launch of the festivities, a fair wind issued off the Brillian Sea and dispatched the clouds racing westward toward the Hun-derian Mountains.

The regent's spring festival began traditionally with a parade through the streets of Valerton. As parades go, it was a humble affair, more of a public procession than anything else. It was led by the regent, Victor Bimm, who wore the ceremonial red-and-gold robes of his office. He was accompanied by Valerton's mayor, Louise Spate, and the president of the Artisan Guild, Stuart Carver. They were followed in close order by a dozen soldiers from the regent's personal troops. (It had been so long since there had been an armed conflict in Korasan, the soldiers were viewed as ornaments of ceremony rather than instruments of power.) Trailing the troops were a variety of civic leaders and minor government functionaries. Behind them marched a mellifluent chorus of schoolchildren.

The parade began outside the regent's hilltop residence, descended along Port Street to the seaside, proceeded past the warehouses and the shipping docks, and wound its way up to Guild Avenue and into Valerton's central square.

Waiting eagerly in the square for the arrival of the parade was an eclectic array of acrobats, clowns, dancers, fire eaters, fortune-tellers, food and craft vendors, jugglers, magicians, and strolling troubadours. There was also a tattooed contortionist, a midget ventriloquist, and an extremely skinny snake charmer. For approximately two hours—from the moment the crowd thronged into the square until the start of the popular whistling competition—these assorted entertainers and opportunists vied for the attention of the several thousand Korasanians, who gawked, shopped, and cheerfully commingled in the square.

Antoinette could see that Lydia was uncomfortable in the midst of so many people, so she took her by the hand and pressed forward through the eddying mass. "Come on. Let's get out of the middle here. I'll show you where the band will play tonight."

"Okay," Lydia replied weakly. Although she was intrigued by the diverse profusion of faces surrounding her, the physical closeness of so many strangers had an unsettling effect on her nerves. After bumping, dodging, and weaving their way forward for several minutes, the girls reached the outer edge of the crowd.

"The stage is just ahead," noted Antoinette, "at the foot of the courthouse steps. There. Do you see it?"

Lydia, being taller than her pert cousin, had seen the elevated platform before the question was asked. "Yes. Is that where they hold the whistling contest?"

"No. Whistling is on the other side—on a stage in front of the archive building," answered Antoinette. Then, concerned about the alienated look in Lydia's eyes, she slipped an arm around her cousin's waist and inquired, "What's bothering you?"

"Nothing."

"Are you sure? You look nervous."

For a second Lydia wished she was back home again, alone in the tranquillity of the familiar Jeefwood Forest. There, at least, she did not have to worry what people thought when they looked at her. There, at least, she knew what to expect. Soon, though, this feeling passed, and Lydia sighed. "I guess I'm just excited. That's all."

"I'm excited too," Antoinette said, "but there is nothing to be afraid of. Now, follow me."

Antoinette led Lydia up twenty stone steps to the courthouse entrance. From there they enjoyed a wide overview of the festival crowd. Using a finger to describe an imaginary circle in the square below, Antoinette explained,

"Later, someone will erect velvet ropes to mark off the dancing area. All along the outside there will be tables and chairs. You have to pay to sit down, but we won't do that. That's for older folks."

"What will we do?" Lydia asked innocently.

Antoinette grinned. "We'll find a spot to stand and pretend like we don't care if anyone asks us to dance or not."

"So that's the tactic." Lydia laughed. Here, high above the crowd, she was beginning to relax.

The girls were interrupted by a teenage boy dressed in all the latest fashions. He wore dark trousers with broad, upturned cuffs, a blue-and-green-striped shirt with an extra-wide collar, and pointed black boots. A cinnamon-colored cap complementing his reddish hair was cocked at an angle on his head. "Hello, Antoinette," he said with a quick bow. "Nice to see you out and about."

"Hi, Edbert," she replied cooly. Edbert Sands was what might be called a rich kid. His father owned several stores (including the seed store above which Aldersan Hale had his studio) and a fleet of fishing skiffs. Edbert was bright and charming, but sometimes he tried just a little too hard to be likable. He also happened to be the boy whom Antoinette had accidentally kissed on the lips.

He was undaunted by Antoinette's icy manner. "That's a fine outfit you're wearing on this fine day."

Antoinette crossed her arms and hemmed.

Edbert took a long look at Lydia, then removed his cap and inquired of Antoinette, "Pray tell, who is this striking creature by your side?"

Lydia blushed and looked around. In the distance she

15

could see someone pulling a wooden cart through the crowd.

Antoinette answered Edbert with evident pride. "She is my best friend and first cousin. Her name is Lydia Swain."

"Nice to make your acquaintance, Lydia," Edbert said with an exaggerated sweep of his arm. "Any friend of Antoinette's is surely a friend of mine."

Lydia nodded but did not speak. Her attention was focused on the fellow with the cart. He was a slim, taller-than-average young man with shoulder-length brown hair. He wore tan pants and a light blue work-shirt. Lydia was intrigued by the patient yet steadfast way he maneuvered through the crowd.

Edbert withdrew a bag from his hip pocket and extended it toward Antoinette and Lydia. "Candied ginger," he said. "A special treat for two special girls."

Antoinette huffed. "You know, Edbert, you are about as corny as they come."

"Only trying to be nice," Edbert said in a defensive tone.

Antoinette smirked before reaching to pluck a sweet nugget from the bag. "Normally I wouldn't, but since it's ginger, I'll make an exception."

"And you?" Edbert offered Lydia the bag.

"Oh . . . no thank you, Edbert," Lydia replied without taking her gaze off the man in the blue work-shirt. As she watched, he pulled his two-wheeled conveyance to the rear of the stage and began removing ropes from its odd-shaped canvas-covered cargo.

"You really ought to try this ginger," Antoinette trilled. "It's out of this world."

"Maybe later," Lydia mumbled.

Edbert popped a nugget of ginger in his mouth and sat on the step below the girls. With a giggle Antoinette reached over his shoulder and took a second piece of candy from the bag. Although she was not willing to admit it, she kind of liked Edbert.

Lydia continued to watch as the young man pulled open the stage curtain and began struggling to hoist his strange cargo onto the elevated platform. His first attempt was aborted when the obscured object nearly tipped out of the cart. He caught it with a shoulder, returned it to an upright position, then stood back and put a hand to his chin. It was evident to Lydia that he was trying to devise a strategy.

Lydia, having a rather practical mind and a fairly well developed mechanical sense, was used to helping her father with various chores. And so—doing what came naturally to her—she descended the steps and offered to assist. Although Antoinette and Edbert were surprised by her action, Lydia did not give it a second thought.

Or rather: Lydia did not give her action a second thought until the young man turned to face her. His brown eyes were bloodshot from working all night on the griffin and there were lines of weariness creasing his forehead, yet she sensed that he was a kind, thoughtful person. He confirmed this by speaking in a tender voice. "Very civil of you to offer. Yes, I could use a hand."

Lydia gestured with a shrug that she was ready.

Aldersan smiled appreciatively. "Okay. If you'll just keep this from tipping over sideways, I'll climb on stage and grab it with these straps."

Lydia stepped forward to place her hands against the large draped object. It was heavy.

"Got it?"

"Yes," Lydia squeaked.

After leaping onto the stage, the young man hooked two straps around the object. He shifted his feet, established eye contact with Lydia, and counted, "One. Two. Three. *Lift.*"

On the first try they managed to hoist the object onto the edge of the stage. Aldersan took a few seconds to wrestle it into a safe position, then looked around to thank his assistant. Much to his surprise, she was walking away. "Hello," he called.

Lydia turned shyly.

"You are very strong."

Lydia blushed. A gargantuan butterfly had emerged from a chrysalis in her stomach and briefly robbed her of the ability to speak.

"It was extremely considerate of you to help. Thank you."

In her mind Lydia muttered the words *You are extremely handsome,* yet her lips said, "You're welcome." Then she smiled with happiness and turned to float up the courthouse steps.

When she rejoined Antoinette and Edbert, the bag of candied ginger was sitting empty between them. Antoinette greeted her with a mischievous wink. "I can see you don't intend to waste any time here in Valerton."

"What?" Lydia asked innocently.

"You know what," countered Antoinette. "Flirting so boldly with Aldersan Hale."

"Who?"

"Aldersan Hale, Valerton's premier artist."

ᕗ3

The archives building sat at the rear of a recessed yard located off the main square. Well before one o'clock a large crowd had filled the space in anticipation of the festival's annual whistling competition. The art of whistling was held in high regard in Korasan, and the coastal region around Valerton was renowned for its great number of talented performers.

Antoinette, Lydia, and Edbert found a place to stand near Antoinette's parents, Ella and Willard Bell. Glenda Swain was backstage with her husband, trying to help him relax. After surviving the morning preliminaries (thirty-eight entrants had been eliminated), Lloyd had drawn number six from the lottery bowl and thus would be the last competitor to whistle. Only moments before, he had decided to blow an old standard called "Blue Moon over Korasan." It was a tricky, up-tempo number filled with key changes, but it was Glenda's favorite and Lloyd felt it might win him the prize.

Louise Spate stepped onto the small stage in front of the

archives building and waited until the crowd grew silent. Then she introduced the judges, read the names of the six contestants, and signaled for the competition to begin.

A freckle-faced farm boy was the first to whistle. He was clearly nervous as he puckered and wet his lips. He began well, but quickly wandered off-key and lost the thread of the melody. After a few embarrassing moments, the boy threw his hands up in despair and stopped whistling. The crowd moaned sympathetically as he lumbered awkwardly off stage.

The second contestant was a cobbler from Valerton. A giant fellow with a timid demeanor, he whistled a simple melody that was well within his range. Unfortunately, on several instances one could hear him gasping for air.

Two down, thought Lydia, and three to go. She knew it was not proper to derive pleasure from someone else's failure, but still, she was encouraged for her father. He had been practicing all year for the event, and she wanted very much for him to win. He had told her privately that he hoped to use the prize money to buy a set of glass goblets for Glenda.

The third contestant was from a small village at the foot of the Hunderian Mountains. Although she was an improvement over the second whistler, she performed a simple dance tune that lacked any challenging passages, and no one really expected her to win.

The fourth contestant was an elderly white-haired man who had won on four previous occasions. Not unexpectedly, he whistled the same complicated ballad that he whistled every year. Today his notes were crisp, delivered in the easy style of someone relaxing at work, and when he was done the applause suggested that he was the front-runner.

As the elderly champion sauntered offstage, it was clear from the pleased expression on his face that he believed he had already won the contest. But a moment later, when the fifth whistler strode forth and pierced the air with a shrill prelude to the classic "Goldeneye," the old man was promptly forgotten. All eyes and ears were now drawn almost magically to the stage, where a tiny girl named Sophia stood wearing a tomato-red dress. She could not have been more than nine or ten years old, and her lungs could not have been much larger than two roses.

Yet size never hampered a songbird, and it surely did not restrain Sophia. With her tiny arms swinging to keep time, she swayed back and forth on her heels and whistled with all the aplomb of a drunken sailor on shore leave.

The audience was mesmerized. Sophia the bird-girl had the sustained vibrato of a violinist and the perfect pitch of a composer. To many of the astonished members of the audience it was as if they were hearing "Goldeneye" from the alluring lips of a siren.

When Sophia ended her astounding performance with a double-octave trill, the crowd erupted in thunderous applause. Although Lydia now knew her father's chances of winning were extremely slim, she clapped with the same abandon as everyone else. Hearing the bird-girl had sent a chill of joy up her spine.

Lloyd's spirits sank when he heard the applause awarded to Sophia. "I can't follow her," he said nervously to Glenda.

"Of course you can," Glenda replied firmly.

"But . . . I . . . I'll just embarrass myself after a performance like that." Lloyd hung his head despondently.

Glenda, understanding her husband's moods, knew what was required at this moment. She stepped forward, wrapped her arms around Lloyd, and whispered in his ear, "Lloyd, you came this far. You have to go out there. Just imagine you are at home in the forest."

"In the forest," he mumbled as if in a trance.

"Yes, deep in the forest," Glenda added softly as she turned her nervous husband toward the stage and shoved him forward.

Lydia beamed with pride when her father emerged from behind the curtain. She was used to seeing him at home in rumpled work clothes—not on stage with his hair slicked back and his shirt tucked neatly in his pants. Suddenly, for the first time in her life, it occurred to her that Lloyd was a rather handsome man.

"Blue Moon over Korasan" is a song that requires a sure ear and a vast amount of concentration. It should not be attempted in public by a nervous whistler. The song begins slowly and sweetly like a lullaby, then steadily picks up speed as it builds toward the refrain. The refrain is not only swift but also filled with full-octave harmonies. After the refrain, the tempo of the song slows again and returns to the original thematic harmonies of the composition.

Lloyd stared blankly at the crowd for an awkwardly long time before wetting his lips and beginning. Glenda sighed with relief as the first notes of the melody cut sharply through the air.

Lloyd's timing was flawless as he approached the refrain, which he proceeded to whistle with clear precision. When the refrain was complete, he paused to take a single deep breath, then skillfully followed the melody line back to its initial cadence. It was an elegant transition. Everyone with ears knew he had captured the very soul of the song.

After Lloyd whisper-whistled the final notes of "Blue Moon over Korasan," the audience exploded with an applause that was as warm and uproarious as the praise they had given the bird-girl.

⊰⥸| 4

The Bells and the Swains had a late-afternoon meal in one of the public dining halls near the square before returning to the Bells' home to rest and prepare for the big events of the night. Lloyd Swain tried to relax, but his efforts were to no avail. Each minute for him passed like an hour, and each hour passed like a day. The results of the competition were scheduled to be announced that evening, just prior to the dance. First Lloyd would have to wait while the regent gave his annual speech to the gathered guild members; then the mayor would read the name of the contest winner.

Although Lloyd's eyes were closed as he lay in bed, and though he made snoring sounds, he only pretended to sleep so that Glenda would quit telling him to relax.

On the floor above, Antoinette and Lydia had put on cotton robes and were sitting at a window watching the setting sun emblazon the distant clouds with color. Antoinette alternated her attention between the sunset and her fingernails, the latter of which she was painting in a rainbow scheme. After a while she sighed. "It's a mystery why they don't hold dances every night."

"A mystery?"

"Yes. It's so exciting getting ready for a dance. If I ran the world, I'd throw one every night."

"Maybe they wouldn't be so exciting if they happened every night," suggested Lydia.

"I suppose you're right." Antoinette nodded, then giggled. "Every other night would be better."

Lydia acknowledged her cousin with a silent smile. The thrust of her attention had turned to the distant clouds. They seemed to be moving slowly toward the coast. Perhaps, she thought, it was the same bank of clouds that had darkened the skies over Valerton that morning. Whatever the case, she was trying to read them for a sign. It was something she often did at home in the forest. Sometimes . . . well, it seemed to her there was much a person could learn from the clouds.

Antoinette studied Lydia's profile. "My dear sweet cousin, what are you thinking?"

At that instant the sun transformed a mauve tower of clouds into an orange pillar of fire. Lydia admired the spectacle for a moment before turning to her cousin. "I was wondering why I hurried away today when that artist tried to speak with me."

"Oh yeah, Aldersan Hale. Maybe it was good you ran away."

"Why do you say that?" Lydia asked curiously.

Antoinette blew on her nails before replying, "Because more than one girl in this town has tried to rope Aldersan Hale. They say it's not so difficult to get his attention, but holding it is a problem."

Lydia did not know what to make of Antoinette's comment. "I thought he was nice."

"I never said he wasn't nice." Antoinette stressed her point with an adamant shake of a green-tipped finger. "In fact, he is *very* nice. He's just . . . well, he's so serious about his artwork that sometimes he forgets what is really important."

"Do you think it was artwork we lifted on stage today?"

"We'll probably find out tonight. Speaking of which, let me see your dress again."

The gold dress that Glenda Swain had made for Lydia was scooped at the neck and had straight, elbow-length sleeves. It was drawn in at the waist with a simple sash, and had a gathered skirt that fell to mid-calf. Glenda had embroidered a copper-colored featherstitch around the hem and neck.

Lydia was so proud of her mother's work that Antoinette did not have the heart to tell her the dress was strikingly out of fashion. Instead, she said, "Very original. You won't have to worry about anyone else wearing the same thing."

"Mom is very creative."

"She is that," Antoinette agreed tactfully, then moved to pat the back of a chair that faced her bedroom mirror. "Sit

25

here, Lydia. Let me see what I can do with your lovely fair hair."

Later, they left the house while the adults were still sipping cider in the parlor. Antoinette had lent Lydia a peach shawl to go with her dress. For herself, she selected a silver scarf to match her form-fitting blue gown.

It was dark now, and the air was heavy with moisture. Lydia's spirits sank a bit when she looked up and saw that the stars were partially obscured by a wispy vapor. Usually that meant rain. But then Lydia recalled that Valerton was a coastal town subject to fog, and her spirits lifted.

The girls hooked arms as they strolled along Guild Avenue. Here and there they saw, drifting in and out of shadows on the lamp-lit sidewalk, other well-dressed individuals, or couples, or small groups, making their festive way toward the dance. For a girl from the deep country, it was all very exotic.

When Antoinette and Lydia arrived at the central square, they could see that a large area at the foot of the courthouse steps had been cordoned off with ropes. Although the Artisan Guild dance was held primarily for the families of the guild members, it was also attended by the public at large. Because of the prosperity the guild brought to Valerton, almost every villager viewed the organization in a favorable light and lent support to its activities. The dance, which was originally held at the guild headquarters, had become so popular that it was eventually moved to the central square. About five hundred people were expected tonight.

When the girls arrived at the plaza, they found the place

buzzing with activity. The night air rang out with the cacophonous sound of craft salesmen, food vendors, and entertainers hawking their services and wares.

"Come on, Lydia. We have a few minutes to spare. Let's look at some of the booths."

"I, ah . . ." Lydia hesitated as a strange, unnameable fear settled over her.

Antoinette saw the reluctance in Lydia's eye. "Just stick with me," she advised her timid cousin. "You'll be fine. Besides, it's not so busy as it was earlier today."

Antoinette made a beeline for one of the jewelry booths, where for several minutes she stared enviously at a display of earrings. "Wow, look at this. Mother-of-pearl set in heart of jeefwood. I wish I was rich."

Lydia sighed and looked around. A few yards away a shirtless man swallowed a flaming sword. She saw in the periphery of his light a contortionist scratching his ear with a toe. Somewhere out of sight a tamborine kept time with a whistling guitar player.

Antoinette eventually tore herself away from the jewelry and hooked arms with Lydia. "Are you hungry?"

"We ate just an hour ago," Lydia reminded her pretty cousin.

"Right. Okay." Antoinette nodded. "So, I suppose it's time we start toward the dance area. We don't want to miss anything."

Between the public area and the roped-off section, there was a dimly lit strip of plaza about thirty yards deep. Without a word, and without unhooking their arms, the girls quickened their pace. Just as they were passing through the middle of the dark strip, they encountered a tall man wearing a high-collared cloak. *Encountered* is putting it mildly: Actually, Lydia ran smack into the man. He stumbled before recovering his balance. The girls were rendered immobile with shock.

They experienced instant relief when the tall, cloaked stranger chortled with amusement, "I suppose that was my fault for getting between two young ladies and a dance."

"We're sorry," Antoinette managed to whisper.

"Please excuse us," adjoined Lydia.

"It's quite all right." The stranger shrugged, then added in a disappointed tone, "I really should have known we would bump into each other. You see, I'm a fortune-teller."

Antoinette forgot her urge to flee, and the curious side of her nature took over. "How could you have known we would run into each other? We decided only a second ago to come through here."

The man shook his head. He seemed quite unwilling to accept any excuses. "It's my profession. I should have known."

Lydia also forgot her fear. She could now see that the tall man was very old, and not in the least bit threatening. "How much to tell a fortune?"

The old man seemed pleased by Lydia's inquiry. "That would depend on the fortune told. If you are a sovereign or a regent, it's twenty-five talens. But if you happen to be a young lady in a gold-colored dress, it's two binks."

Lydia turned to Antoinette, who shrugged as if to say, *You decide.* Lydia opened and felt around in the little purse she was carrying. All she found was a comb and her ticket for the dance.

"Or . . ." The old man paused to weigh his words. "If you don't have any binks, it's free."

"Really?"

"Yes, really," the man confirmed his offer. He then grew somewhat righteous as he explained, "I'm not in the fortune-telling business for the money. I tell fortunes because . . . well, because I enjoy telling them. I charge people only because they seem to appreciate it more when it costs them money."

"I could pay you later," Lydia offered meekly.

"Nonsense, my dear. What is your name?"

"Lydia Swain."

"Well, Lydia, we were thrust together for a reason. Let us go into the light and see what the future holds for you."

The trio walked toward the roped-off area where a ring of torches shed a flickering yellow light over the north end of the square. After the man found a spot suitable for divination, he spread his cloak and sat cross-legged on the cobblestones. The girls stood silently, watching intently as the curious stranger withdrew a jeefwood box from an inner pocket and gently shook its contents. He mumbled something in a language the girls did not recognize, set the box on the stone pavement, and then lifted his gaze to Lydia. Returning to the normal tongue of Korasan, he spoke in the manner of someone sharing a secret: "The future is for the making"—the old man smiled cryptically—"and for the very well made. For all of us there awaits a good future or a less-good future. The purpose of life, of course, is to pursue the good future, and the instrument for doing so is belief. Lydia, if you believe what you believe, even when you have forgotten why you believe, then one day you will arrive at the good future that already awaits you."

Lydia looked at the seer and indicated with a nod that she accepted his words, even if she did not fully comprehend them.

Slowly, with reverent concentration, he lifted the box from the pavement and handed it to Lydia. She was startled. It was hardly heavier than air, and it seemed to tingle in her fingers.

"Lydia, when you are ready to learn what the future may hold in store for you, rattle the box and set it down."

After glancing at Antoinette, whose expression revealed that she was mesmerized by the proceedings, Lydia closed her eyes. Then she shook the box and placed it on a cobblestone.

The old man bent over until his face was within inches of the box. He tapped it three times and whispered something in a secret language. The lid flew open. Lydia and Antoinette exchanged astonished glances. When they recovered, they looked down and saw that the inside of the box was lined with purple velvet. Lying upon the velvet were seven cubes carved from bone. A single hieroglyph was inscribed on each of the six surfaces of each cube. The seer peered quickly at these symbols, then closed the lid and returned the box to a hidden pocket in his cloak. He did this so swiftly that the girls saw only a blur of movement. Suddenly he was on his feet, staring into Lydia's expectant blue eyes. When he spoke, it was in a thin voice that sounded older than the beginning of time. His words came slowly. "I see a sleeping stranger. I see a stormy sea. I see the sovereign sighing. Behold! There is a kiss beneath a jeefwood tree."

It was clear that the divination had cost the old man a great amount of physical effort. He shuddered and bent forward to rest his hands upon his knees.

Antoinette, who had been uncharacteristically silent until now, knew she should wait for the old man to catch his breath before pestering him with a question. But she did not wait. Her curious side had taken over again. "That's very interesting, but what does it all mean?"

The fortune-teller raised a brow at Antoinette and replied flatly, "It means whatever it means. My job is to read the future—not to interpret what it signifies."

"Oh," Antoinette said with some embarrassment.

The old man suddenly seemed to regain his vigor. He became a towering figure once more, then cocked his head and stared at the speechless Lydia. In a warm voice he informed her, "One by one, you will see these things and the meaning will become clear."

Lydia pursed her lips to speak but held her words. She had the feeling that the old man was reading her thoughts.

The tall seer smiled at some private inner reflection, then bowed respectfully to Lydia. He dipped his head at Antoinette and began to shuffle away from the light.

He had gone about twenty yards when Lydia found her voice. "Thank you," she cried.

The old fortune-teller glanced over his shoulder and waved before fading mysteriously into the shadowy strip.

Lydia stood stunned as she watched the dark area into which the seer had retreated. She could hear his words reverberating in her mind. *I see a sleeping stranger. I see a stormy sea. I see the sovereign sighing. Behold! There is a kiss beneath a jeefwood tree.* Although she had not a clue as to how any of this might relate to her own good future, she felt a thrill of excitement at the possibilities they suggested.

She was jolted from her reverie when Antoinette grabbed her arm and exclaimed, "Nothing like that has ever happened to me."

Lydia sighed ponderously. "He was very nice. I wish I had thought to ask him his name."

"To heck with his name. You should have asked him what your future meant. I mean, really—a kiss beneath a jeefwood tree. It sounds very promising to me."

"Hmmm," hemmed Lydia.

"Come on," Antoinette chirped. "We have a dance to attend."

⇥5

The regent Victor Bimm was a plump, wide-shouldered man with heavy jowls and steely gray eyes that were constantly on the move. He had dark hair, which he wore in a spiraling pompadour that pointed

out over his broad forehead. Even without the plush ceremonial robes he was wearing, it would have been apparent
to an uninformed bystander that he was a very important
person.

As Lydia listened to the regent's speech on the necessity
of expanding Valerton's economic base, she could only
marvel at the man's oratory skills. His movements were
small, his manner relaxed, yet his voice swept over the
crowd with the resonant power of a choir. It seemed to
Lydia that if Victor Bimm had wished to do so, he could
have persuaded everyone to walk down to the docks and
jump in the sea. The logic of his words almost did not
matter; it was their delivery that held his listeners in
sway—or rather, most of his listeners. What Lydia did not
know was that anyone who had done business with the
man had learned to hear his words with suspicion. This
distrust ran especially deep in the hearts of the guild
leaders, who knew the regent was envious of their influence with the general public.

Waiting patiently in a semicircle on the stage behind
the regent sat the members of Korasan's most popular
dance band, Tommy Brill and the Nightingales. Resting in
the center of their arc was the canvas-draped object that
Lydia had helped hoist onto the stage. She, as well as
everyone in the square, was quietly curious as to what was
under the canvas. The only person not eager to see the
object unveiled was Aldersan Hale. He, at this moment,
crouched in a corner at the rear of the stage.

In keeping with his skills as an orator, the regent knew
how to read his audience, and he was aware they had come

to dance—not to hear a lot of political flapdoodle. He soon wound his speech toward a conclusion: "What is good for business is good for the people. So in order to help our region in realizing its full potential, I have devised an economic plan that will elevate the prosperity of everyone here. The details are in the process of being negotiated, and I shall announce them when they have been completed."

The regent wore a humble expression until the moderate applause died. (Anyone watching the crowd closely would have noted that no guild officers bothered to applaud.) After a moment he smiled and pointed to the object at center stage. "I suppose you are wondering what is under the canvas." A murmur from the crowd endorsed his supposition. "It is a gift I commissioned for the Artisan Guild. It was created by one of their own, Aldersan Hale." Another murmur arose; this one of a distinctly supportive nature. "Aldersan, come forward and stand with me."

Emerging reluctantly from his corner, Aldersan walked shyly past the band members and stood behind the draped griffin. He looked handsome in the brown vested suit he wore, but his face said clearly that he did not enjoy appearing before the public. His discomfiture doubled when the crowd burst into applause.

As friends, family, and fellow members of the guild whistled and clapped their support for Aldersan, he fidgeted awkwardly and looked vainly about for a place to hide. The regent wore a smug smile, privately congratulating himself on his political astuteness for commissioning such a well-liked native son.

After the cheering subsided, the regent grabbed a handful of canvas and prepared to lift it from the obscured griffin. "And now," the regent announced in a booming voice, "to be placed in the lobby of the guild headquarters, I give to you this symbol of my unwavering devotion to the general economic welfare of Valerton."

A symphony of ooohs and ahhhs wafted over the square as the grand jeefwood sculpture was revealed.

Lydia hardly noticed the griffin. She was distracted by the distinct impression that Aldersan Hale was staring directly at her. Of course, being surrounded by a dense mass of people, it was difficult to assess the validity of her perception. Even so, her fluttering heart was convinced.

It was evident from its reaction that the crowd approved of the grand griffin, yet the regent seemed less than pleased. Contrary to his desire for a dominant and fierce creature, the animal on stage seemed somehow gentle and wise, and totally lacked the intimidating aura he had hoped it would project.

Although the signs of Victor Bimm's displeasure were subtle, they were not lost on Aldersan Hale. If there had been a hole anywhere on stage, Aldersan would have found it and escaped. As it was, his fidgeting grew more desperate than before.

Several workmen hustled forth when Victor Bimm signaled for the sculpture to be removed. Being a man of heightened political instinct, he restrained himself from criticizing the artist in public. (He would demonstrate his displeasure when Aldersan requested his final payment.) The tension broke a moment later, when Louise Spate stepped forward with an envelope in her hand. The regent took this opportunity to bow before the crowd and exit stage left. Aldersan Hale winced, then exited stage right. The musicians cast sympathetic glances at him as he scurried past; they had also noted the regent's displeasure.

For a mayor, Louise Spate was an exceptionally attractive and likable individual, and she received a sincere welcome from the gathered citizenry.

Lydia craned her neck to look for her mother and father. They were at a table located on a landing to the left of the plaza floor. They sat with the Bells and two other couples. Lydia could see—even at a distance and in the uncertain light of torches—that Lloyd was tense with suspense.

"Greetings," the mayor cried. "Before the dancing begins, I have the pleasure of announcing the winner of Valerton's sixty-eighth annual whistling contest." A whir of anticipation arose from the crowd as the mayor tore open the envelope. Lydia held her breath. "This year," Louise Spate piped excitedly, "for the first time in the history of the event, we have a tie. The joint winners are . . . Sophia Quirk and Lloyd Swain."

Louise Spate tried to say something about where to collect the prize money, but her words were lost in a howl of cheers.

Lydia thought she might faint with happiness, yet before she had the chance to swoon, she heard Antoinette speaking at the top of her voice. "Hurry, Lydia. Let's find a good spot. We're standing on the dance floor. We have to move to the side."

Lydia, giddy with the news that her father would share first prize with the bird-girl, could not stop grinning as she followed Antoinette toward a coveted step at the edge of the plaza. For the moment her anxieties were forgotten. Rather than feeling estranged from society, she now felt as if she were a small part of a happy whole.

Just as Antoinette and Lydia secured a spot on the desired step, a workman passed by with one end of the velvet rope that defined the dance area. Antoinette took it as a matter of pride that they were now perfectly positioned. She was just about to gloat on her successful maneuvering when Edbert Sands appeared at her side. Though he tried to pretend that the encounter was a coincidence, both Antoinette and Lydia knew it was the outcome of strategic action.

"Hello, ladies," Edbert greeted the girls with the surprised look of an amateur actor. "Fancy meeting you here." Then, with a look of sudden awe, he added, "Antoinette! What a gorgeous gown! I must say, blue becomes you."

Before Antoinette had the opportunity to express her opinion of Edbert's theatrical talents, Tommy Brill and the Nightingales struck up the first tune of the night.

As the musicians plucked, strummed, beat, and blew upon their instruments, Tommy Brill crooned into a standing megaphone that dispersed his rich voice evenly over the square. Lydia watched with growing delight as the first few couples sauntered into the dancing area and began moving to the music. Although Antoinette had given her a lesson earlier in the evening, Lydia knew she still had lots to learn. While some couples made dancing seem easy, others made it appear to be the most difficult thing in the world. After observing for a moment, Lydia concluded that mastering the movements of dance had much to do with picking the right partner. Or in her case, she reflected, being picked. This insight did little to comfort her. In fact, it filled her with an inexplicable dread and opened the door to the closet that held all her personal anxieties. She steadily went from analyzing the mechanics of dance to agonizing over whether anyone would ever invite her to try. Already she had noticed three different boys glance in her direction, yet not a one had deigned approach. She wondered if it was her dress that stayed their interest. Or was it her hair? Or was it . . . her face?

Meanwhile, the fashionably attired Edbert Sands persisted in his efforts to persuade Antoinette to dance with him. Finally, at the beginning of the fifth song, when the plaza had become thick with swinging limbs, she relented.

Lydia wanted to be happy as she watched her pert cousin twirl round and around with Edbert, but the truth was she had never felt more awkward or more alone in her life.

Couples laughed gayly. Somewhere someone in the crowd harmonized with Tommy Brill. One song melted easily into another. Dancers flowed in and out of the inner square. Lydia did manage to grin when she saw Antoinette press a quick kiss upon Edbert's cheek (his look of surprise would have honored the finest of actors), but her smile was soon supplanted by a down-turned look of dashed hopes. Time, she felt, was running against her. The big night was passing her by.

Lydia bit her bottom lip when Tommy Brill announced that the Nightingales would play one more song and then pause for a twenty-minute break. By this point she was ready to give up. If she could have had her wish, she would have been back home in the sanctuary of her favorite forest grove, or in the garden nursery tending her sprouting jeeflets. There, at least, she would have her loyal dog Walter to keep her company. There, at least, she would not feel so alone.

Earlier in this story reference was made to an old saying that beauty is in the eye of the beholder. Sayings such as this are known as clichés. In defense of clichés, it should be noted that they do not earn this distinction without bearing a certain grain of truth. With this in mind, reference is now made to a cliché stating that the darkest hour comes before the dawn.

Just as the dejected Lydia was about to break down in tears, she felt a tap on her arm. When she turned, Aldersan Hale was at her side. "Hi. I've been looking all over for you."

"For me?"

"Yes." Aldersan smiled at the look of astonishment on Lydia's face. "I wanted to thank you again for helping me today. I'm Aldersan. What's your name?"

"Lydia."

"Pretty name. Would you care to dance?"

Lydia tried to speak, but it would not be honest to label the sound that came out of her as an actual word. Effectively, though, it was a yes.

Aldersan ushered Lydia to an opening in the sea of

couples. She felt like she was floating in a lovely dream. Suddenly he stopped. He placed his right hand on the small of her back and clasped her right hand with his left. Instinctively Lydia rested her left hand on his shoulder. Sideways she stepped, then backward. Sideways, turn, then forward. Sideways and turn. Before she even registered the fact, she and Aldersan were dancing.

Not only were they dancing, but they were dancing smoothly. Time, instead of running against Lydia, was now running with her. The music accompanied her like an old friend. Sideways, turn, sideways, then forward again.

Lydia saw Antoinette signaling happily in her direction, but she did not wave back. That would mean removing her hand from Aldersan's shoulder. Instead, she winked at her cousin. Sideways and forward. If only the music would last forever.

But of course the music did not last forever. Tommy Brill hummed, the drumbeat ceased, a trumpet blew the final note.

Aldersan took his hand from her back. "You dance very well."

"Thank you." For the first time Lydia looked straight into Aldersan's light brown eyes. "I didn't even know I knew how."

"You could have fooled me. I thought you were an expert."

Lydia blushed happily.

Although Aldersan did not actually blush, his face was tinted with warmth. "I regret it was such a short dance."

"Me too," Lydia agreed.

Aldersan sighed and shrugged, then said, "Perhaps the two of us might dance again when the band returns?"

"Oh, could we?" Lydia blurted excitedly.

Aldersan was amused by her exuberance. "If you say yes, then I promise we shall dance again."

"Yes."

Aldersan lifted his right hand and declared in a solemn tone, "Lydia, I give you my word that we shall dance again."

Lydia stared at Aldersan yet did not say a word. Her glimmering eyes expressed her complete concurrence with the notion of dancing again.

"Now, please excuse me," said Aldersan. "I have to help the workmen mount the griffin on its pedestal."

Lydia replied with a nod. She was afraid that if she opened her mouth, she might whoop with joy.

Aldersan shook her hand gently before departing. "I'll look for you where I found you the first time."

During the intermission Antoinette and Lydia went to say hello to their parents. Lydia had just finished congratulating her father on the results of the whistling contest when the first rumble of thunder reverberated in the west. With a sinking feeling Lydia recalled the clouds she had seen at sunset.

Initially there were just a few isolated droplets of rain . . . but that was initially. In no more than a minute after the first rumble of thunder, the rain was pounding on the

41

rooftops like an army on the move. When the storm hit the square, it hit like a monsoon.

Quite soon, even the most optimistic of optimists gave up hope and started running for cover.

⊰א 6

The downpour that brought an abrupt end to the Artisan Guild dance continued unabated through the night and began to let up only at dawn. It was still drizzling after breakfast when Lloyd Swain went to fetch his team of horses from the stable.

Late that morning, when the Swains said their adieus to the Bells, the drizzle had ceased, but the skies remained heavily overcast and gray. As she had done on the journey to Valerton, Lydia rode alone in the rear of the wagon, huddled in a corner under one of her mother's quilts. Unlike before, when the wagon had bumped and creaked along the old wooded lane, it now swayed and groaned over a wet, grabbing surface. Lydia's mood, like the muddied lane, was substantially altered from what it had been two days before. Now, instead of thinking ahead with high hopes and giddy expectations, her thoughts trailed behind in melancholy review. She was not feeling blue because her visit to Valerton had been a disappointment. To the contrary, her thirty-six hours in the village had surpassed her wildest dreams; she was feeling blue because the visit was over.

Lydia was not the only Swain lost in a reflective mood. In spite of the lingering positive effect of having tied for first place in the whistling contest, Lloyd Swain was pensive. He had been prompted to serious musing by a rumor he had heard the night before. He kept reminding himself it was a rumor—an unverified speculation, at best—yet he knew he was only looking for excuses to mitigate his apprehension. After all, the fellow who had shared the rumor was none other than Stuart Carver, the steadfast and eminently respectable president of the Artisan Guild.

"Lloyd, Lloyd." Glenda nudged her husband with an elbow. "Quit acting like a lump on a log and whistle me a song."

"Gee, honey," Lloyd moaned reluctantly. To him it seemed as if his whole way of life was threatened. If the rumor about the regent's economic plan was true, then trouble was on the horizon. For as long as anyone could remember, jeefwood had been exported from Korasan only as a finished product, but now (if the rumor was true) Victor Bimm was preparing to revoke the guild's exclusive control over the precious tree and rule that it be sold as a raw commodity. The mere thought of jeefwood milled into lumber was enough to turn Lloyd's usually strong stomach.

"Whistling will make the trip go faster," Glenda noted.

"Haven't you heard enough for one weekend?" Lloyd had not yet revealed his troubles to Glenda, and she had not asked about them. She knew he would tell her when he was ready.

"No," Glenda said firmly. "I haven't heard enough

whistling for one weekend. Besides, the horses like it when you whistle."

"Gee, honey," Lloyd repeated with a small shrug. Although the forest he managed was controlled by the Artisan Guild, it was owned by the sovereign, Sa Viddledass. He was the noble yet slightly disengaged ruler who lived in the town of Finngastoot, which was located on a peninsula in the south of Korasan. Sa Viddledass was truly benign. On his own he would have never meddled with guild business; that just organization had been successfully established for too long to warrant interference. In many ways, the Artisan Guild was a model union, benefitting equally both its members and the community in which it was based. But then the sovereign was not the problem. The problem was his appointed representative in northern Korasan. Unfortunately for the guild, whatever the regent declared became law.

In the darkness of his imagination Lloyd was terrified that if jeefwood lumber was offered for sale on the world market, his forest would rapidly be reduced to a collection of ugly stumps. The guild's conservative policy of strictly limited jeefwood harvests not only guaranteed the existence of healthy forests for future generations, it also ensured a stable market value for guild products. What frightened Lloyd almost as much as the image of a denuded forest was his knowledge that the guild would go down fighting before such a tragedy was permitted to happen.

"Don't *gee, honey* me." Glenda nudged her husband for the second time in five minutes.

Lloyd's smile, though weary, was full of affection. He had never learned how to resist his wife's wishes, and he

44

was not ready to start learning now. He drew a deep breath, licked and puckered his lips, and began to whistle an old ballad called "Tickle Me with Tenderness."

Sure enough, soon after Lloyd started to blow, the horses whinnied in appreciation.

Lydia hardly noticed the coming of twilight. Although she had spent the entire day recalling each detail of her adventures in Valerton, she was still too preoccupied with her review to notice something as routine as dusk. In her mind she had gone over each scene at least ten times, and by this late hour she had turned to counting and categorizing her experiences. By her calculations she had slept for nine of her thirty-six hours in the village. That left twenty-five waking hours, ten of which were spent gabbing with Antoinette in her third-floor bedroom. Of course, these ten hours with her cousin were of some measurable value, but nothing actually occurred during their passage, and thus they were less pertinent than the remaining fifteen hours. Out of these hours the essential story of her trip was told. And in the telling there were a half-dozen experiences that combined for a total of seventy-seven minutes. There were the ten minutes she watched Aldersan pulling his cart through the crowd; the seven minutes during which she helped him hoist the griffin onto the stage; the twenty minutes she had passed in the presence of the fortune-teller; the eight minutes during which she and Aldersan danced (these were particularly glorious); the two minutes spent talking afterward; and, finally, the half hour she, Antoinette, and Edbert had stood in the pouring rain, hoping in vain for the band to return.

Night was about to swallow the lane when Lydia was drawn from her reveries by a familiar yapping sound. It was Walter, waiting obediently at the gate. (Lydia had trained him never to leave the property without a chaperon.) As the wagon drew near, he stood on his hind legs and barked with unrestrained mirth.

Lydia jumped to her feet when she heard Walter's joyous outcry. "Oooh. Good boy. What a good boy!"

The brain of a normal canine has difficulty grasping the concept of calendar time, and Walter's noggin was no exception. Although Lydia had explained before her departure that she would return after three days, he had not understood. In fact, he had feared the Swains would never come back. So now, when he heard Lydia calling him a good boy, he got so excited he yelped and turned a back flip. Unfortunately for the little fellow, his joyful histrionics were curtailed by a loud honking noise. That was Weezie. Her wings were spread wide and she was charging toward the gate as fast as her webbed feet would propel her.

Walter took off quicker than a rabbit avoiding an interview with a fox. He would be redeemed later, after the Swains had unpacked the wagon, checked on their seven sheep and three cows, and retired to the confines of their cozy cottage. They would call him to come join them by the fireside, and when this moment arrived, Walter would turn at the door and give Weezie a haughty, superior look that clearly stated *Dogs, but not geese, are welcome inside.*

The cottage where the Swains lived had been built more than two hundred years before by one of the first guild foresters. Although his name had long been forgotten, the product of his labors continued to stand strong against the hands of time. The cottage, erected with jeefwood and stone, was basically a square, four-room abode. Typical of houses in Korasan, it was designed around a grand kitchen with a brick bakery oven.

A good home is like a reliable friend, and every veteran traveler knows that returning to one after an important journey has its special rewards. A mere minute after opening the door to her room and espying her familiar bed, Lydia had undressed and fallen fast asleep.

During the night Lydia dreamed she saw the regent riding a griffin through the streets of Valerton. Then, in a blurred shift of images, the griffin was transformed into a stallion ridden by the fortune-teller. She waved to the old seer, and when he turned to reply, she saw that it was actually Aldersan Hale mounted upon the horse. Instead of waving, he held his right hand up in the manner of a solemn oath.

Lydia awoke in the morning to the contented mooing of three cows grazing in the yard outside of her window. They were happy because Glenda had returned to relieve the milk pressure from their udders, and to feed them corn. Lydia climbed from bed and went to the window. She blinked after pulling back the curtains. The sun was shining brightly in a cloudless blue sky. It's high spring, she thought. First-summer is almost here.

She changed into a pair of overalls and hurried to the kitchen. There she wolfed down the porridge her mother had left on the table. Then she rinsed her bowl, placed it in the washtub, and dashed out the door. A strange new feeling had emerged in her heart, and she was eager to reflect on the feeling before it faded. First, though, she wanted to check on her jeeflets to see if any new seeds had sprouted while she was away.

Walter, having been put out earlier, was anxious for Lydia to make an appearance. When she finally did step outside, he crawled from under the shed that served as the garden nursery and wagged his tail, then stood by the door while Lydia went inside.

Her four jeeflets in clay pots by the south window were doing fine. Lydia sprinkled water on their budding leaves, then turned to her seed tray. When she removed the cover of burlap from the tray, she found one seed swollen and cracked—a good sign that it was about to sprout—but in the others she saw no change. She poured warm water in the tray, lay the burlap over the seeds, and exited the shed.

It was time now to examine the strange new feeling in her heart, and the obvious place to do so was atop the lichen-covered boulder in her favorite forest grove. Actually it was not a grove but just a clearing in the forest that Lydia loved. The boulder sat directly in the center of the clearing. Lydia's best ideas always came to her when she was lying on her back atop that boulder, gazing skyward through an opening in the canopy of jeefwood leaves.

Until an individual has spent idle time meandering in the company of jeefwoods, he or she has not experienced this planet's finest hour. Indeed, anyone who does not know the charms of a jeefwood forest cannot fully estimate the genius of nature. One tree alone is enough to incite awe. There is no other life form on Earth that lives as long, grows as large, or exudes the same noble aura. It is possible that somewhere in the depths of the great oceans there may exist a creature—a giant squid, perhaps—to rival the magnificence of a mature jeefwood, but as of this writing, no such being has ever been documented.

Jeefwoods, in the beech family of trees, often live for more than a thousand years. Given the proper conditions, the tip-top of a jeefwood will reach four hundred feet. Such a specimen might have a trunk five yards thick at the base, and its lowest branch may protrude from a spot fifty feet above ground. They have dark green ovate leaves that are attached to their branches by ropelike petioles. Although the leaves fall off at irregular intervals and later replace themselves, they never fall all at once, and thus the jeefwood is not truly deciduous. The tough, crenulated bark of the tree is of a reddish, brick-brown color. It is a fruit-bearing plant. Once every five to ten years each tree produces a single yellow flower that slowly transforms into a gigantic black seed encrusted in a dense, waxy pod.

Just as someone who has not meandered through a jeefwood forest cannot imagine its beauty, neither can that person imagine the sheer scope of the forest. Even in what would constitute a tight cluster of jeefwoods, the trunk of one tree would not be nearer than forty feet to the next. For a human, the proportions in such a woods can be overwhelming.

This was the world in which Lydia had grown up. It was the space she knew and loved. And yet today—although not a leaf in the forest had fallen during her trip to Valerton—it was a world that had changed dramatically.

(Anyone following her experience closely might surmise that it was the world inside of Lydia that had changed, not the one without.) While Walter sat contentedly in his usual spot at the base of the boulder, she lay atop the rock with her eyes closed. A part of her mind listened to the murmuring breeze, yet the bulk of her brain ruminated on her own good future. The fortune-teller had implied that her good future was already in place, just waiting for her to arrive. She would find it, he said, by believing in what she believed. As Lydia soon realized, believing what one believed was easier said than done . . . or at least it was in her case. To begin with, she had strong instincts about many things, but she was at a loss when it came to articulating her exact beliefs. Indeed, she was not even sure how to distinguish between the thoughts in her mind and the feelings in her heart.

Lydia lay thinking for several hours, until eventually she grew so confused trying to separate her thoughts, she sat up and screamed. Walter awoke and began to bark. He had presumed that something was attacking Lydia, and he wanted to let that something know that he was there to defend his mistress.

"Calm down, little fellow," Lydia said with a laugh. "It's okay. Nothing has happened."

Although Walter understood the spirit of Lydia's words, he decided to err on the side of caution. He huffed himself up like a great big dog and trotted fearlessly around the boulder.

Lydia did not know why, or how, but she sensed that the world had changed again. Perhaps the catharsis of her scream had tilted the balance, or maybe Walter's loyal protestations had altered a frequency. Whatever . . . all she knew was that she was suddenly free from a fog of excess analysis. And as the mists cleared, she could hear again the natural voice of her own heart. It remembered how to know things without stopping to scrutinize each bit of knowledge. It reminded her that she knew what she knew.

She stretched and peered upward into the green canopy. Two things she knew made her smile. The first was that Aldersan Hale had raised his right hand and sworn, "Lydia, I give you my word that we shall dance again." The second was that the mysterious fortune-teller had said, "Behold! There is a kiss beneath a jeefwood tree."

7

After returning from the spring festival, Lloyd began an exceptionally busy period of work in the Jeefwood Forest. He was preparing for the arrival of first-summer, when the men from the Artisan Guild would come with their wagons for the annual harvest. He had already chosen the two jeefwoods he intended to recommend for the taking. Still, there was much to be done. Each day, following the performance of numerous morning chores, he took his climbing gear and went to prune selected limbs from some of the older trees. This was slow and dangerous work. After each limb was culled, he trimmed away the smaller growth and gathered it neatly in mounds. Afterward he carted the felled limbs to one of the drying sheds behind the cottage.

For Lydia, driven by the feeling that the world had somehow changed around her, the days and weeks after the spring festival marked the beginning of a troubling period in which she became painfully aware of her social isolation. Never before had she felt bored or unhappy with her solitary life in the Jeefwood Forest. But now, after a taste of the village, the daily routines that had once absorbed her interest lost much of their previous luster. Watching clouds was no longer so entertaining, and her old habit of taking long, exploratory hikes through the woods lacked much of its former appeal. Even the option of assisting Lloyd, which she often did (he was convinced that his daughter had an advanced aptitude for working with tools and machines), seemed tedious and dull. And so, as the usually cheerful and easily content Lydia pondered the pleasures of a life that was not hers to lead, time began to weigh heavily on her soul.

Time: the big boss that imposes its authority upon all matter, in every dimension. It is the head honcho that eventually masters everything in the universe. Or almost everything. For some inexplicable reason, time is occasionally foiled by the machinations of the human heart. Yes, that foolish little muscle, the heart . . . crazy enough to pit itself against time. And though it never actually defeats the clock, it does not always go down in utter defeat. Indeed, when the heart is strong, it is often willful enough to bend the big boss's rule.

As the passing days became weeks, and then a month, Lydia peered back and forth through time so often that time itself seemed to grow confused and wander through the forest in circles. When peering back, she repeatedly returned to the moment when Aldersan Hale had found her at the dance and said, "I've been looking for you." When peering forward, she searched through the unknown for signs of her own good future.

Poor, sweet, isolated Lydia . . . living in the remote woods without the possibility of a chance encounter with the slender, brown-eyed artist of her dreams. Although she was not by nature a complainer, nor the type to pity herself, some days she felt so lonely and so far removed from the march of life in Valerton that she felt as if she might break down and cry. In her mind she lamented: "Why am I left out? Why can't I have the life of a normal person?"

Growing bluer by the day, Lydia journeyed back and forth through time . . . back and forth . . . until eventually she came to the conclusion that there was nothing for her to do but pray.

Every culture that has ever existed has contained some element of spiritual teaching near, or at the core of, the belief systems that define the culture. The urge to understand the hidden world is universal to all people. Religion, for the most part, is an attempt first to gain such an understanding, then to express and integrate that knowledge back into the culture from which it has sprung. Ideally, the religion of a place reflects the moral and philosophical beliefs of the people it serves. Occasionally there are multiple religions serving a variety of separate groups existing within a single culture. Sometimes religion leads and the people follow; other times the relationship is reversed.

Compared to other cultures, Korasan is rather unusual. A strong spiritual influence pervades the land, yet there exists no organized religion to interpret and perpetuate this influence. Korasanians (for the most part) simply know that it is the individual's responsibility to behave with moral integrity and good will to others. As a people, they do not require ecumenical leaders to remind them of this duty. Generally, they accept that there is much about life that is, and will always remain, a mystery. If asked about their beliefs, typical Korasanians might say they believe there is a God in heaven attended by a hierarchy of angels, and a few might mention the existence of a celestial orchestra; but this is all proper Korasanians will usually say about the matter. If pressed for further details, they are apt to recommend that you go figure it out for yourself.

It took a full four weeks for Lydia to do so, but in the end, she did figure it out. She may not have had all the intellectual glitches examined to the last detail, but she did resolve the issues where they mattered most—in that foolish little muscle called the heart. One day, while she was sitting on the boulder in her favorite forest grove, the solution simply came to her. When it did, she turned her gaze upward and directed her hopes to heaven: *Please, I know you are up there. Hear this prayer, that Aldersan Hale is healthy, and see that he remembers his promise to me. Please, if you will be so kind, look down and make these things come true. Please, answer my prayer.*

Lydia had no mental image of any particular entity to whom she sent her prayers (she did not imagine an ethereal being with wings, nor an omniscient face with a white beard), yet she did feel that she was addressing a friendly spirit.

On the night of the day that Lydia directed her hopes up to heaven, some fifteen leagues north and east of the Swain's cottage, Aldersan Hale stood alone in his drafty studio above the seed store in Valerton. The full force of his attention was focused upon the large cylindrical chunk of jeefwood resting upright on the pallet before him. After taking a special vote, the directors of the Artisan Guild had given Aldersan the wood as a bonus for his consistently fine work at the factory. He was immensely appreciative. He had never before sculpted such a sizable piece of the precious commodity. His respect toward the material was so great, it was almost reverent.

It was three weeks before the first-summer moon, and Aldersan, like most other guild workers, was on vacation until after the annual jeefwood harvest. So tonight, having the right piece of wood and twenty-one days at his disposal, he was preparing to begin the greatest challenge of his artistic career. Now, for the first time ever, he was getting ready to sculpt a full-sized human figure.

Softly and deftly, with his lightest hammer in hand, he tapped at the heel of a handmade chisel. He was making the initial cuts around what would ultimately define the head of the figure. At this point he was still searching for the character of the wood. He was listening and watching, trying to discern the intrinsic spirit of the material. He

55

knew from experience that if he was receptive enough, the wood would find a way to speak to him. It would speak silently and abstractly, in an obtuse voice that only an artist might hear or comprehend. . . . Still, it would communicate. Eventually, he knew, the interior figure that was locked within the material would reveal itself. This was the way of the sculptor's art—to find what was hidden and bring it into the light. It was more than work. He was not executing a commission. He was not carving a knickknack. Tonight Aldersan was beginning a search for the ineffable spirit that would elevate the wood beyond the physical representation of an object. He was hunting, so to speak, for an unknown animal that lived in an unknown world.

Although a sharp eye and a steady hand were valuable assets, Aldersan knew that the trick of his art—of making something that would surpass contrivance—was to listen and then remember what was heard. As of yet he had not determined the age or sex of the figure; he knew only that he was searching for a human form. And so he *tap-tap-tap*ped lightly upon the chisel, then stood back to listen.

Meanwhile, on the south side of Valerton, in the back room of a warehouse by the sea, Stuart Carver was conducting a secret meeting with some of the guild's higher-ranking members. The subject of their gathering was the pending announcement of Victor Bimm's economic plan. For the past month it had been a source of much worry for the guild leadership, and now there was a certain urgent feeling among many of the men that some counteraction be taken. A spy in the regent's household (one of the maids, who shall go unnamed) had informed Stuart of

Bimm's intention to make his announcement at first-summer—a time when nearly half of the guild members are away for the jeefwood harvest.

Although Stuart Carver's attempts to meet with the regent and discuss the guild's concerns had been foiled by a series of evasions, he nevertheless counseled a calm response to the perceived threat. "I agree that neither our guild nor our forests would survive the open sale of jeefwood, but I also believe that an open conflict with the regent is to be avoided if possible. Before we decide to challenge the man directly, we would be wise to consider thoroughly all the alternatives."

The opinion of those gathered was that preparation for a worst-case scenario would not be imprudent. "What you say is true, Stuart," said Vassal Pender, the guild's accountant. "But the fact is, we've been considering our options for four weeks now . . . and I think it's time we prepare for the inevitable. Bimm has ten guards at his house and perhaps another twenty at the western garrison, while we have more than thirty able-bodied men among our ranks."

Bash Landy, a lathe operator, stood and shook a chubby finger. "I say we arm ourselves now."

Stuart frowned thoughtfully. "No sense in fighting a fire that hasn't started yet."

"Perhaps," allowed Malcomb Belt, a designer. "But it does make sense to fill your water buckets before the flames appear."

"I'm with Malcomb," shouted Bash, who was still standing. "We should be ready to defend ourselves."

"Gentleman, restrain yourselves," urged Stuart. "It is not yet definite that there will even be a conflict."

"Knowing Victor Bimm, there will," mumbled Dale Hands.

Aldersan Hale's father, Craig, stood and cleared his throat. "Tell us, Stuart. If the regent does sign a contract to sell jeefwood to foreigners, will we be able to contest him in court?"

"Unfortunately, our legal options regarding formal decree will be limited," Stuart explained. "We might be able to petition the sovereign."

"Bah," booed Bash Landy. "Petitions are for politicians. Force is the way to state our objections."

"Sit down, Bash. You're always itching for a fight."

"Maybe now is the time to scratch."

"Gentlemen, gentlemen. Nothing has happened yet."

"Aye. But surely something will."

"God save the jeefwood tree."

In this somewhat disorderly yet democratic fashion the meeting continued long into the night.

The post rider who traveled the old road from Valerton to Finngastoot each week usually passed by the Swains' cottage near midday on Monday. On this, the fifth Monday after the spring festival, Lydia was waiting for the rider. She was hoping for a reply to the letter she had sent Antoinette two weeks before. The rider smiled when he saw Lydia sitting by the gate. He stopped his sorrel mare beside the gate, withdrew a pink envelope from his satchel, and stretched to hand the letter to Lydia. "This is for you. Pardon my reaching like this. I'd dismount if it weren't for that wicked goose of yours."

"Weezie?" Lydia giggled. "She isn't wicked."

"No?" The post rider smiled dubiously. "Even so, I'm not getting down."

Antoinette's letter contained little real news. She did write that she had gone sailing one afternoon with Edbert Sands, but otherwise her missive was limited to incidental anecdotes and gushy endearments. Much to Lydia's chagrin, Antoinette made no mention of Aldersan Hale. Still, it was nice to receive a letter, and later that evening Lydia scripted a reply. Her letter was also lacking in any real news. What could she say?

Dearest Antoinette, Lydia began. *My life is so boring. There is absolutely nothing to report. Nothing ever happens here. All I have to do is daydream about my future.*

In the coming days, Lydia arose early each morning, dressed quickly, gobbled breakfast, checked on her jeeflets, and headed straight for the forest. After settling atop the boulder in the clearing, she would begin her daily review of the half-dozen scenes that told the story of her trip to Valerton. Those eventful seventy-seven minutes remained as fresh as the air around her. In her mind the village remained just the way it had been during the spring festival. (She did not know of the tension that was mounting between the Artisan Guild and the regent. She had noticed that Lloyd was unusually preoccupied in thought, but she attributed this to nervousness over the upcoming jeefwood harvest.)

After completing her review of the festival weekend, Lydia gazed up to heaven and whispered a variation of the entreaty she had been whispering each day for the past week: *Please hear this prayer. I know you are up there. Please see that Aldersan Hale is healthy and remind him of his promise to me. Won't you be so kind as to look down for a moment? Won't you make these things come true? I ask you, please, answer my prayer.*

After making her appeal, Lydia stretched, sighed, and began daydreaming about her own good future. From time to time she glanced skyward and concentrated: *I know you are up there.*

Lydia's words were born in her heart, and it was there that she felt them resonate. Mentally she had no expectations of a response. She never really considered whether she was actually getting through to heaven or not; she only knew that it felt good to pray.

Please, answer my prayer.

⇥ 8

F ar above the small nation of Korasan, high in the sky, beyond the causal and the astral planes, in the lower reaches of heaven, the angel Ebol was growing restless. It was that girl. She was praying again. Why he could not turn her off he did not know. Of all the supplicant humans on Earth, why was he hearing her so clearly? This was the seventh day in a row that she had disturbed his nap. And not just once a day—but twice and thrice, or four times, or more. Such impertinence! Where were the girl's manners? Was it no longer possible for an angel to get a good day's sleep?

Ebol yawned and put his palms together. He turned on his side, laid his right cheek upon his clasped hands, and tried to get back to sleep. He had almost done so when he heard the words *Answer me. I know you are up there.*

Many individuals, when they die, go to heaven, but it is a precious few who become angels. That is an honor reserved for a select handful of truly generous souls. Earning the wings of an angel is quite a serious matter.

This is not to suggest that every angel is . . . well, a perfect angel. Not all are sweet and soft and full of shimmering grace. In fact, some angels, like the humans they once were, are given to a vast array of moral quirks and personality foibles. Some are a tad vain, others are mischievous, and a few, like the angel Ebol, are less than enthusiastic about their cosmic duties.

Truth be told: The angel Ebol was a sleepyhead who had pretty much been snoozing nonstop throughout the two centuries since his soul had matriculated into the celestial hierarchy. Once a month or so he would arise to wander around heaven, catching up on all the latest gossip, but he was never awake for long during these jaunts, and afterward he always rewarded himself with an extended slumber.

Of course, the reader must make allowances for the influences of Ebol's environment. He was, after all, in heaven, and everyone knows there is nothing so delicious as heavenly sleep.

But now Ebol was awake, and try though he did, he could not block out the sound of Lydia Swain's appeals. It was as if she were aiming her entreaties directly at him. Hmmm. He begrudgingly accepted that he was not going to fall back asleep anytime soon. Grumbling, he got up and began to pace. What, he wondered, was so important about the content of this girl's prayer? It seemed like a simple, straightforward request. There were no fires to fight, no dragons to slay. Any good angel worth his weight in moonbeams ought to be able to answer her. Why, Ebol wondered, was she disturbing *his* tranquillity?

Curiosity eventually got to Ebol. Against all his better instincts, he exercised a fundamental angelic power and peered down through the atmosphere. Now, where? Ah, yes, Korasan. In the great Jeefwood Forest. Hmmm. Let's see. The cottage, the garden, the sheds. Now . . . across the field and into the woods. There! There she was . . . sitting on that boulder in the small clearing. About sixteen, he guessed. Of all the luck! It would be a teenager who disturbed his heavenly sleep.

Just then Lydia glanced up and thought, *I know you are up there. Please, won't you look down and answer my prayer?*

Ebol heard her appeal as clearly as if she were shouting in his ear. Though he was less than thrilled by the situation, he had to admit she was putting her heart into her prayers. Perhaps that's it, he thought; perhaps I hear her so clearly because she speaks from the heart and reveals a potential for touching upon the true feeling.

To an angel, the true feeling is the key to everything. It is the quality that honors a soul and places it in the celestial hierarchy. The true feeling cannot be faked; it occurs when, and only when, one soul cares purely for the welfare of another soul, and then acts in an unselfish manner for the benefit of that other soul. All angels know that the unselfish act is a prerequisite for the acquisition of wings. Following strict rules of moral conduct on Earth does not guarantee anyone anything. Granted, good behavior helps a soul rise toward heaven, but to become an angel, one must first experience the true feeling.

Although Ebol thought it probable that Lydia was touching upon the true feeling in her prayers, he was not considering her as a candidate for angelhood. For one thing, he was just a basic angel, and selecting qualified applicants for the celestial hierarchy was not his job. (That important task was the bailiwick of the virtues and the dominions, who then submitted their recommendations to the thrones.) And for another thing, well . . . Lydia was not deceased. To the contrary, she was very much alive. In fact, if Ebol was reading the fabric of her daydreams correctly, she had quite a future yet before her.

Now that she had awoken him and drawn his attention, Ebol began to develop a keen interest in Lydia. He had been snoozing so much in recent decades that he had forgotten how fascinating it was to observe humans leading Earth-bound lives. From his point of view, they all seemed so earnest and serious about what they expected from life . . . so wildly impassioned and idealistic about their dreams. It was certainly true that Lydia had this intensity, although in her Ebol thought he detected something uniquely genuine and soft. No, not soft: strong.

Or rather, soft and strong, and flexible like a wind-blown tree.

As Ebol leaned forward, peering down through the atmosphere at Lydia, the angel Natalie floated over to his cloud and stood behind him. "Hi there, Ebol," she said, nearly scaring him out of his wings.

"Natalie!" exclaimed Ebol. After the startled look faded from his face, he began to glower.

The angel Natalie was undaunted by Ebol's furrowed brow. She met his glare with an innocent grin. "I'm so delighted to see you decided to wake up this year."

Ebol started to say something critical, then caught himself and shook his head dubiously. He knew Natalie well enough to know that words would never change her. Although she had been only twelve when she ascended into the celestial hierarchy and thus retained many childlike characteristics, she had been dwelling in heaven long enough to establish herself as an engaging force. Even the dominions knew they might as well try to convince the devil to be good than try to suppress Natalie's ebullient personality. "Okay, so I'm awake," Ebol conceded with a long face. "But I'd be asleep if it were not for some pleading teenage girl down in Korasan."

"Ah," sighed Natalie. "You've been called."

"Yes . . . I suppose so." Ebol shrugged with dispirited resignation.

"Teenagers make the best believers. Smart enough to know, yet unburdened by the soul-stifling disappointments of adulthood. It's a shame the way age fills a human with blinding doubts."

Ebol acknowledged Natalie's comment with a nod. Although he had arrived in heaven as a sixteen-year-old boy, he was not particularly fond of teenagers. "Apparently this one has no doubts at all. She keeps saying she knows I'm up here. And I'm telling you, she's persistent."

"Aren't they all?" Natalie retorted with a knowing smile as she bent to peer down though the clouds. "Go ahead, Ebol. Bring her into mind. I want to have a look."

Ebol's reluctant grimace went unnoticed by Natalie. He felt like kicking her, but of course, being an angel, he did not move his foot. Instead he leaned forward and brought the Jeefwood Forest into focus.

After a moment Natalie remarked, "Oh, yes. I see her sitting on that boulder."

"It's her spot," Ebol noted.

Dusk was falling over the mortal world as Natalie and Ebol looked down upon Lydia. It may be that Lydia sensed the divine attention, or perhaps she was simply putting in a last prayer before the end of the day, but for whatever reason, she chose this moment to send up another appeal: *I know you are up there. Please, won't you hear my prayer, that Aldersan Hale is healthy, and see that he remembers his promise to me?*

"She sure comes through clearly," exclaimed Natalie.

"Too clearly, if you ask me," Ebol moaned.

As they watched, Lydia slid down off the boulder and started for home. Walter trotted proudly and closely at her heels.

Natalie turned with a beaming smile. "You know, of course, that when they come through so clearly, it means they are touching on the true feeling."

"Yeah." Ebol nodded. "I thought that might be the case."

"Oh, look!" Natalie pointed. Weezie was hiding behind a bush near the path. As Lydia and Walter strolled within striking range, she burst forward with her wings spread. Walter skedaddled faster than you could say "Blue Moon over Korasan."

After Natalie recovered from laughing, she sat down on Ebol's cloud and asked, "So, who is this Aldersan Hale? And what promise did he make to her?"

Ebol glanced plaintively at Natalie, then lowered his gaze and shrugged. "I don't know. I haven't looked."

"Shame on you, Ebol." Natalie shook a finger. "You are going to have to answer her, you know."

"You just wait a second," Ebol cried in a somewhat righteous tone. "Who are you to shame me and tell me what to do?"

The angel Natalie grinned yet did not say a word.

Ebol saw that Natalie was not going to be easily dissuaded. He also knew in his heart that she was right. "Well," he muttered defensively. "I ah . . . I just woke up a little while ago."

The angel Natalie began to giggle. "You better get busy, then. After you have been called, the longer you procrastinate, the more complicated your mission becomes."

"Holy gamoly!" Ebol swore under his breath.

Natalie's giggle exploded into a musical laugh. "I hope you aren't afraid of geese."

In heaven there are no rules. There is only respect for the true feeling.

9

There is no better season in Korasan than the weeks leading up to first-summer. Each night in Valerton the streets and cafés are filled with the happy sounds of Korasanians relaxing in the soft breezes that stir almost constantly off the Brillian Sea. For the young and the young at heart, late spring is rich with distracting pleasantries and sweet promises. Everyone goes out strolling at night—that is, everyone except the infirm, couples stuck at home with babies, the psychologically imbalanced, and the working artist.

Below and beyond the walls of his studio, Aldersan Hale could hear the occasional sound of someone calling to a friend or the faint murmur of people laughing together. Although he was quite human and drawn to society as a whole, to him the sounds were like so much water falling over a distant dam. They provided a context against which he juxtaposed his existence, but he did not allow them to distract him from his labors.

Actually, on this night, it was unlikely that Aldersan would have been distracted by a riot. After nearly a week of tentative tapping and listening for a voice in the jeefwood, a person had begun emerge. The shoulders had come first, round and sleek, then a slender neck, and afterward the curved cheekbones of a woman's face. It was a young woman. Now, as he carved the slightly crooked line of a narrow nose, he began to have the vaguest sense that he recognized the face. Yet who? Who was this girl emerging from the block of jeefwood? Dimly, in the back of his questioning mind, he knew that he knew her. But from where?

Let go, he reminded himself. Let go and listen.

Unbeknownst to Aldersan: As he stood studying the mysterious sculpture, he was being watched over by the angel Natalie. Having taken a vicarious interest in the Lydia Swain case, Natalie had decided to conduct her own investigations, and the first thing on her agenda was to locate the object of Lydia's prayers. Natalie did not intend to involve herself directly in the matter, but rather was acting out of concern for Ebol. She did not wish to see him shirk his first call to duty and thus doom himself to an eternity of silence.

Natalie observed Aldersan for several nano-instants, then rushed over to Ebol's cloud. Not surprisingly, he was snoozing. Natalie, being the irrepressible soul that she was, felt no qualms about rousing him from his slumber.

Just as Aldersan was unaware of what was going on above, he was deaf to the activity in the street below. "Hey, wait for me," cried the voice of a young man. It was Edbert Sands.

"I'm waiting already. But do hurry," Antoinette replied impatiently.

Edbert finished retying his shoelace and sprang to his feet. "Okay. I'm ready now."

"You know, Edbert, if you bought a pair of sensible shoes, the laces wouldn't come untied every ten minutes."

"I thought you said you liked them."

"Hmph." It took Antoinette a moment to find a reply. "I said they were good-looking; I didn't say whether I thought they were practical or not."

Edbert groaned and shook his head. "You sure are difficult to please."

Antoinette turned with a dramatic flair, her face forming a mask of wounded feeling. "Well then, Edbert, if you think I'm difficult to please, perhaps you should cease trying."

"Perhaps I should," Edbert muttered sourly. Inside he was chuckling; he knew Antoinette had a convoluted way of expressing her affection.

Meanwhile, across town, on Valerton's highest hilltop, in the jeefwood-paneled dining room of the regent's residence, Victor Bimm was supping in private with Felix Drump. Felix was a shipping magnate who had arrived in Korasan that very evening. He was from the island of Zapin and was reputed to be one of the wealthiest men in the world. He and Victor had been corresponding for over a year. Tonight was the first time they had ever met.

Victor Bimm waited until the last of the dinner plates had been removed and mead was served before broaching the matter that had brought Felix Drump to Valerton. The meeting was critically important for Victor. He understood clearly that the success of his venture depended upon his having Felix's cooperation, and his awareness of this dependence made him uneasy. Of course, being a man of high office, Victor was practiced at veiling his true emotions. He leaned back casually in his upholstered chair, passed his nose approvingly over his mead goblet, and aimed a knowing, familiar smile at Felix. "So, my friend, I am encouraged by your presence at my table. Pardon me if I seem presumptuous, but I do not suppose you would come all this way if you were not interested in making a deal. I hope you find my proposed terms reasonable . . . if not actually a little generous."

Except for the controlled lift of an eyebrow, Drump did not immediately reply. (He had not grown rich by letting people read what was on his mind.) He waited until the regent began to show certain subtle signs of nervousness, then took a long, deliberate sip of the fine Korasanian mead. After setting his goblet on the table, he muttered with cool ambivalence, "Yes, the terms."

Victor Bimm had anticipated Drump being a shrewd negotiator, and he had pondered long in preparation for this meeting. He knew that some businessmen were irresistibly attracted to profit, and he was hoping that Drump was such a fellow. "Of course, Felix, we will want to discuss the fine points of my terms, but I ought to tell you now, my percentage figures are nonnegotiable."

"Everything is negotiable," Drump said with an enigmatic smile.

Something about the magnate's manner alarmed the regent. The man had not challenged the proposed figures, yet already Victor sensed that his bargaining position was beginning to weaken. He attempted to restore his perceived loss by reminding his visitor, "The whole world wants jeefwood. It is a very precious commodity. It is also a fact that anyone wishing to trade in jeefwood must do so through Valerton. And he may do so only with my blessing. Of course, you would have the exclusive shipping rights. At twenty-five percent of gross, you would soon be a rich man."

"I'm already very rich," Felix noted with a sardonic snort. "Even so, let us imagine that we can eventually agree on a proper division of the gross. What guarantee do I have that you can deliver a steady supply of jeefwood to my ships?"

Victor Bimm could feel beads of sweat gathering under his collar. He had not yet worked out the details of harvesting and hauling the jeefwood. "My word should suffice as guarantee. It is, after all, the law in this part of the country."

Felix Drump was not impressed. He had done his homework, and he knew it was probable that the open sale of jeefwood would meet with stiff resistance from the Artisan Guild. "Oh? How do you enforce your law?"

"Excuse me?" The regent had not anticipated this line of thinking.

Felix smiled patiently at Victor, then calmly elucidated his principal concern: "It is expensive to operate the type of ships required to haul logs across the sea. If there is trouble with your law, how many troops are at your command to ensure that my ships do not sit idly in your port?"

Victor Bimm made a face to suggest that Drump was worrying over milk that would never spill. "Korasan is free from that kind of trouble. Everyone obeys the law here."

The wealthy magnate stared coolly at the regent. "How many troops?"

"Sixty," Victor Bimm lied.

Felix Drump frowned. "Odd you should say that. My scouts count half that many."

Victor clutched at his goblet and suppressed the urge to argue a false claim. With an effort he remained calm. "Thirty soldiers are more than I should ever need."

"Let us hope so." Drump nodded. "Yet if you had twice as many soldiers, you might never need to employ the half that you do have."

The regent swallowed. "What, may I ask, are you suggesting?"

Felix Drump's voice was steady and clear. "For a fifty-fifty split of the gross, I am prepared to lend you thirty of the world's best-trained soldiers. They are waiting now on my yacht."

"Fifty-fifty!" the regent blurted. "That's . . . robbery."

Felix Drump took a long, gratifying sip of mead and smiled. "You should be thankful for my generosity."

At the same moment that Victor Bimm fidgeted in his chair and considered his theoretical losses and gains, Stuart Carver was on the other side of town, pacing anxiously in the parlor of his home. Earlier that evening the unnamed maid who worked for the regent had reconfirmed that Bimm intended to announce his economic plan at first-summer. Only fourteen days remained until that date.

Watching Stuart pace were four of the guild's staunchest

members: Vassal Pender, Malcomb Belt, Bash Landy, and Craig Hale. Pressing heavily on their consciousness was the image of Felix Drump's tremendous yacht. Its presence in the Valerton harbor made the guild members more than just a little uneasy.

Eventually Stuart quit pacing and turned to face the gathered company. "As much as I am reluctant to act hastily, I must admit that if we wait for the regent to move first, we lose our advantage in numbers. Regrettably, it appears as if the time to mobilize has come."

"Good thinking, chief," said Bash.

Stuart acknowledged Bash with a forlorn shrug, then turned his attention to Malcomb Belt and Vassal Pender. "First thing in the morning I want the two of you to visit Lloyd Swain and tell him about the regent's maneuvering. Bimm may send troops out to the forest, and I want Lloyd to . . . well, I want him to know what is going on."

"Right, Stuart," said Vassal. "We can't leave Lloyd in the dark."

"He's a good man," adjoined Malcomb. "He ought to know all."

"It would probably be wise," Stuart added gravely, "for both of you to stay for a few days. That way someone will be available to report back here if there is any suspicious activity."

"Right, Stuart."

"Until further notice, the harvest remains as scheduled."

"Right."

Stuart's expression was fraught with grim concern as he

turned to Bash Landy. "Go ahead and contact your friend. And don't argue over prices. Ample cash will be made available from the guild coffers. Even if we never use them—I pray we don't—it may benefit us to have weapons at our disposal."

"Yes, sir." Bash saluted. He clearly agreed with the guild president's decision.

Stuart moved to lay a hand on Craig Hale's shoulder. "I will need your help writing a letter to Sa Viddledass. If we do oppose the regent, the sovereign should have fair notice that we are not revolting against him."

"I believe Sa Viddledass is a man of reason," noted Craig.

After a pause, Stuart added with guarded optimism, "Perhaps we can persuade him to revoke Victor Bimm's authority."

By horse and wagon the trip from Valerton to the Artisan Guild's grand Jeefwood Forest can take anywhere from six to ten hours. The time will vary with the condition of the road, the condition of the horses, and the temperament of the driver. However, unburdened by a wagon, in fair weather, a person riding a high-spirited steed can make the same trip in three hours or less.

Malcomb and Vassal left Valerton shortly after dawn, and by late morning they were standing next to Glenda Swain, peering up to where Lloyd dangled from a limb. Lloyd stopped whistling and looked down when Glenda called his name. "Darn if it isn't Malcomb and Vassal." He grinned with evident pleasure. "Come to see if I am ready for the harvest?"

"No, Lloyd." Vassal Pender shook his head.

"No question about that whatsoever," remarked Malcomb.

"Honey," Glenda called, "you better come on down now. The men have a message for you from Mr. Carver."

In a flash Lloyd sensed that the men bore bad news. As he looped a length of rope around the bole of the tree and began his descent, he already suspected that the rumor he had heard at the spring festival was true.

When Lydia returned to the cottage for lunch, she saw her father sitting on the rear porch with the visitors. The dour look on Lloyd's face suggested that something serious was amiss. Lydia greeted the visitors with a shy dip of the head before entering the cottage. She found Glenda in the kitchen, kneading dough. A mere glance at her mother confirmed Lydia's hunch that something had gone wrong.

"Mom, what's happened?"

Without turning, Glenda replied, "So far, nothing. Not yet."

"Not yet?" Lydia echoed her mother's words. "Then what is it that might happen later? Something is wrong."

Glenda hesitated for a long moment before answering. She wanted to be honest with Lydia, but at the same time she was reluctant to alarm her daughter. "No one knows what will or will not happen, but there may be a problem with the guild."

"Has Dad lost his job?" Lydia asked anxiously.

"No, dear," Glenda said reassuringly. "The problem, if it comes to pass, is between the guild and the regent."

"What?"

Glenda sighed pensively, then nodded in the direction of the back porch. "Later, when he is ready, your father will explain."

Before Lydia could ask another question, the world was suddenly rent with barking, honking, and hurried movement. Lloyd's voice soon rose above the ruckus. *"Lydia, come out and restrain your goose before I strangle the crazy bird."*

❧10

As much to humor Natalie as to satisfy his own curiosity, the angel Ebol directed his gaze into the studio above the seed store and took a long look at Aldersan Hale. Then he bid Natalie a polite adieu, yawned lazily, and lay back down on the fluffy cushioning of his cloud. All the recent activity was making him sleepier than ever. As it is true on Earth, it is true in heaven: Rest is a natural reward for work. In Ebol's mind (no one ever accused of him of overachievement) the act of peering down at Aldersan Hale qualified as a bit of angelic work. And so, in the guilt-free spirit of a farmer after a dawn-to-dusk day, Ebol closed his eyes and drifted toward a much-deserved slumber.

He had hardly begun to snooze when the voice of Lydia Swain began to resonate in his ear. He tried at first to shut out the sound, but soon realized the futility of this endeavor. Once she had ahold of his ear, it seemed, he had no choice but to listen. Reluctantly he sat up and moaned, then peered down into the now familiar Jeefwood Forest. A moment later he recoiled in shock: What! Modifying her prayer? What sort of impudence was this? Did she really have the audacity to alter her original request?

The night before, after hearing her father's pessimistic prognosis of the recent turn of events in Valerton, Lydia had gone to bed in tears. Several times during the night she had brushed against the realm of sleep, but on each occasion the weight of her anxieties had prevented her from entering that restful dimension. Finally, before the first glimmer of dawn, she had gotten dressed and hurried from the cottage.

Poor Walter. He never saw Lydia leave. (He had been dreaming of goose-liver pâté when she ran by his hiding place beneath the garden shed.) Later, he would spend half of the morning watching the back door, wondering what in the world was detaining his mistress.

Lydia climbed atop her boulder as the first light of day was hitting the tips of the jeefwood trees. She sighed, turned her gaze to the morning sky, and concentrated: *Please, hear my prayer today. I know you are up there. I beg you, please help the Artisan Guild save the jeefwoods.* Lydia paused before adding: *And if it is not too much to ask, while you are doing these things, will you please see that Aldersan Hale is healthy.*

" 'Too much to ask'!" Ebol twitched his wings and muttered sarcastically. "Oh no, my dear Lydia. Nothing is too much to ask of me. You just say the word and I'll jump.

Really, dear, just think of what you want and I'll see that your bidding is done. And please, for goodness' sakes, don't hold back. You won't be imposing a bit. I mean, if your heart desires something, just send up a prayer to Ebol."

Even as Ebol was complaining about Lydia's presumptuousness, another part of him recognized the veracity of her latest appeal. The prayer had been expressed politely, it was concerned with the well-being of others, and it had been rendered with the true feeling in her heart.

The heart again: One would think that bold little muscle would be content to pump blood through the circulatory system. Or if this all-important distribution of the life force did not satisfy its urge to perform, then surely its occasional bouts with the big boss of time should fulfill its duty roster. But *no*, the heart was unwilling to accept limits. If there was something it truly wanted, it was also impetuous enough to grapple with the very shape of the world in which it throbbed.

Where the heart ever found the gumption to behave as it sometimes did, no one—not even an angel—could fairly say. Ebol had no explanation for the phenomenon. All he knew for sure was that Lydia's heartfelt prayers rang in his ears like a clarion call and that sooner or later he was bound to respond. As the meddlesome yet well-meaning Natalie had so succinctly reminded him, "After you have been called, the longer you procrastinate, the more complicated your mission becomes."

In spite of his reluctance to involve himself in the Lydia Swain imbroglio, Ebol had great respect for the true feeling. He was, after all, a member of the celestial hierarchy, and he had not attained that august position by pretense or trickery. He knew what it was like to act on behalf of another.

Ebol had been sixteen when he responded to a flash of the true feeling and performed the compassionate act that earned him his wings. Although the events of his transcendence had occurred some two hundred Earth years ago, he could recall the moment as if it had happened the day before.

An only son, Ebol was the youngest of three children in a farming family that lived on a fertile plain near the mouth of the great Line River in Yegopt. Except for a curious penchant for sleeping at odd times during the day, there had been little about Ebol to distinguish him from other Yegoptian boys living in that time and place.

From the beginning, Ebol's life on the delta had been more or less a matter of daily routine. In the mornings he attended intelligence instructionals at the Sun-Ra Academy, and in the afternoons he fished, or played, or napped along the banks of the Line River. Day in and night out, the seasons of his life passed by like a pleasant, slow-growing habit.

In the mortal world it is sometimes a harsh and immutable fact that individual habits are shattered by exterior forces of change. In the summer of Ebol's sixteenth year, Yegopt was invaded by a horde of bloodthirsty Serpians who roared across the borders from the north. Overnight the rhythms of Ebol's easy existence were disrupted forever. When the Serpians came within a five-hour march of the mouth of the Line River, Ebol's family fled for the coast. There his father swapped his life savings for five spaces on the deck of a departing junker-ship. One morning Ebol had awoken in his old, familiar bed, and the next morning he was watching the sun rise over the Alantean Ocean.

The hurried journey his family made to the coast had been Ebol's first taste of life beyond the delta. All during that first day on the junker-ship he sat in awe of the seemingly infinite expanse of the ocean. When he was not staring at the horizon, his attention was absorbed by the many strange and frightened faces clustered around him on the deck. One young woman in particular caught his attention. About a year older than Ebol, her belly was swollen in anticipation of a child. She was obviously not from Yegopt. Yegoptians, as a rule, are diminutive in stature, with olive complexions, whereas this woman was tall and fair haired. Also, she had cobalt-blue eyes. Ebol had never seen a human with blue eyes before, and he had never seen anyone more beautiful. Each time he glanced in her direction, she was standing alone at the rail, watching the spot where Yegopt had last been visible. The look on her proud face was one of deep anguish. He had never imagined that anyone could be so sad.

Later one of Ebol's sisters conversed with the pregnant woman. Ebol learned that the woman was the wife of a Farroupe nobleman who had come to Yegopt to study the stars. The husband and wife had separated for a few days while he went into the desert with his stargazing instruments, and that was when the Serpians invaded.

That night the junker-ship sprang a leak and began to take on water. A cry of alarm rang out. Everyone on deck scrambled to secure a place in one of the five lifeboats that were hastily lowered into the ocean. So wild and hectic was the movement of humanity reacting to the calamity that Ebol could not recall exactly how he had come to stand on the prow of a small dinghy. It began to move from the sinking ship before he had time even to wonder where the rest of his family had gone. Suddenly a woman's scream caused one of the men controlling the dinghy to halt its movement. It was the Farroupe nobleman's wife. "Please, will you make room for me?" she cried. "The other boats are full."

"This boat is full to the brim," someone shouted from the rear. "There is no more room."

"Please. Have mercy for my child," the woman pleaded though her tears.

"Go, woman. This craft is full. Be quick and see if someone else will take you."

Wild with desperate fear, the woman cried, "Please . . . it is not for me, but I must save this baby."

Suddenly a small voice called from the prow. It was Ebol. He had been hit with a flash of the true feeling. It surged through him like a fire consuming a dry scarecrow and prompted him to act without hesitation. When he acted, he was no less surprised by his own words than were the other passengers in the dinghy: "Stop. Hold the boat steady. I'm getting out. Give the woman my place."

"Are you crazy?"

"That's good of you, lad."

"Hurry then. Make it fast."

Ebol steadied the dinghy with one foot and swung his free leg onto the rapidly sinking junker-ship. Meanwhile someone extended a hand to the woman taking his place. As they brushed past each other, the grateful mother-to-be peered deeply into Ebol's eyes and declared, "May God bless you, my savior. Your goodness will be remembered for centuries to come."

While Ebol floated in the dark water, he could feel the woman's blue eyes watching over him. He would never forget those eyes. After less than an hour, the water began to froth around Ebol. The last thing he saw on Earth was the open jaws of a great white shark.

There was no time to fear or feel pain. The next thing Ebol knew, he had been transported into the domain of heaven. Although he did not realize to what degree he was being honored, there to welcome him was none other than that paragon of all celestial beings, the holy seraph Charlotte.

Of course, Lydia had no idea that she had gained Ebol's attention. She did believe there was an entity above capable of hearing her, but she did not assign any expectations to that belief. Basically, she was following the promptings of her heart when she prayed. It was all that she could think to do.

As the angel Ebol gazed down at Lydia and reminisced about the old days on Earth, he began to accept that he would soon be returning to the mortal dimension of wants and hopes and dreams. With a pang he realized that he missed the world of the living. It had been such a short part of his over-all existence, but oh, how strangely sweet did his mortal memories suddenly seem to him. Oh, how strong his sudden desire to feel the pull of gravity and know the touch of solid things. Now, for the first time in two centuries, he recalled what it felt like to be human. He remembered, of course, that humans often experienced pain and disappointment. Nevertheless he longed to walk again in the tangible world of people.

Please, hear my prayer. The regent proposes to fell these jeefwoods and destroy the Artisan Guild. That must not happen. Please, help save the working people.

Yes, thought Ebol, she prays for others. She has the true feeling. And she needs me. I've been called.

He stood and stretched his wings. Ah, such a pleasure to be awake and feeling decisive. Yes! Now that he knew what he must do, he felt as grand as a well-fed cherub. Of course, there was only one thing to do. He would climb the Karmatic Stairway, waltz into the ninth level, and obtain an audience with the seraph Charlotte. She would grant him permission to descend to Earth.

Charlotte will understand, thought Ebol. I will present her with the merits of the Lydia Swain case, and while I am doing so, I will not be intimidated by her all-consuming fire. So, just as soon as I awake from a fortifying nap, I'll climb that stairway and tell that flaming, six-winged entity exactly what I intend to do. Hold on, Lydia. I'm coming.

᠕ II

Six weeks had passed since the guild dance, one week had gone by since Stuart Carver instructed his associates to prepare for a conflict with Victor Bimm, and now only seven days remained before the scheduled harvest at first-summer moon.

It was late at night. Except for a tapping sound emanating from above the seed store, the village of Valerton was as quiet as a cat stalking a mouse. Aldersan Hale put down his carving tools and plopped wearily onto the studio floor. He had gotten very little sleep during the past two weeks.

Compounding Aldersan's weariness was a frustration with his own lack of artistic clarity. He knew it was a woman emerging from the wood, but who? So far he had managed to balance two chiseled cheeks, set a small chin above a slender neck, define the nose, suggest the shape of the lips and place the eye sockets where they belonged. But who? Who was she? In his mind women were as varied as the stars in the sky, and without a clear sense of who, exactly, this woman was, he was an argonaut lost at sea on a starless night. The artist in Aldersan would not let him rest until he understood the emerging sculpture.

As he squinted in the flickering light, he could feel the quietude of Valerton hanging over him like a blanket of dreams. It felt as though the sleep-master Morpheus had stolen into his studio and begun tugging on his eyelids. His brain sent a signal through his body: Lift me up and carry me home to bed. He started to rise, but something in the wood stilled his movement. Just a moment more.

Be quiet and listen. Then . . . finally, he heard what he had been waiting to here. A voice was coming from the heart of the jeefwood. His patience had produced fruit. It was a feminine voice, tentative and soft. "For me?" it whispered. "I didn't even know I knew how." He sat forward in a state of pitched emotion. After a silent pause, the voice spoke again. "Oh, could we?"

With an almost urgent desperation Aldersan hunted through an array of images stored randomly in back of his mind. I know I have heard that voice before—but where? Then, striking him like a flash of lightning, a name formed on his lips: *Lydia.* It was the girl who had worn the home-made dress to the dance . . . the girl who had helped him with the griffin. She had been so sweet and shy, so different from other girls. And he remembered that he had promised her another dance.

The laugh that cascaded out of Aldersan was essentially an outpouring of relief. (Startled by the sound, a dozen mice scurried for cover.) After his laughter died, he struggled to his feet and mumbled, "The wood has spoken. She has revealed herself. Now I'll make some progress. But first—home to get some rest."

He stepped into the silent street and filled his lungs with fresh sea air. Ah! How joyfully relieved he felt, now that the jeefwood had spoken. What a pleasure to leave his work behind and stand idly in the empty street. He lingered happily for a while, and then, instead of turning right toward home, he allowed a whim to direct him left along Guild Avenue.

As the muffled echo of Aldersan's footsteps bounced lightly off the sleeping buildings, he tried to recall what he knew about Lydia. It was not much. She had not told him her surname. Just Lydia. He was almost certain he had never seen her before the day of the dance, and he knew for a fact that he had not seen her since. Still, having the eye of a figurative artist, he did remember her face. It was long and thin, with chiseled cheeks and a narrow nose that sat slightly askew. The mouth was small and the eyes were a clear blue. Though it was not a face that one could fairly call cute, it was definitely in the registry of natural beauty.

Aldersan passed over the summit of Guild Avenue and began a predawn descent toward the seaside. Now that he had recalled the features of Lydia's face, he felt a strong desire to study it further. But where could he find her? How might he manage to see her again? He continued walking for several blocks, and his musing intellect made a string of deductions: She is a farm girl. She made a special trip into Valerton from the countryside. That explains the homemade dress and her unsophisticated demeanor. That is why I have never seen her in the village before.

A faint hint of morning was tinting the sky as Aldersan rounded the corner of Guild Avenue and Port Street. Yawning, his tired eyes drifted lazily over the dimly lit harbor. He froze. Anchored in the distance was a large boat, and though it was hard to see in partial light, it appeared as if a number of people were disembarking and coming ashore in small punts. At the same time, the large boat turned and headed out to sea.

As the punts drew closer to shore, Aldersan was struck by an impression that the people in the punts were wearing uniforms. Soldiers? he thought. *That's strange.*

With the caution of a thief, he quickly ran down Port Street and hid in the doorway of a warehouse. As the upper arc of the sun poked over the horizon, he was able to count four punts, each carrying seven figures. His heart skipped a beat. It was evident from their trim-fitting drab-green uniforms that the twenty-eight soldiers were not from Korasan. Sa Viddledass's men always wore baggy red-and-gold outfits—just as the troops assigned to the regent did.

Aldersan was incredulous as he watched the soldiers hide their punts in a clump of reeds and assemble on the beach. A hand signal was given, and then, with notable efficiency, the soldiers formed an orderly column and began to jog up Port Street. He shrank back into the depths of the doorway and held his breath. As the soldiers ran past him, a stolen glance at their rounded faces confirmed that they were indeed foreigners.

Forgetting that a half hour earlier he had been ready to keel over from exhaustion, Aldersan began to follow the mysterious troops. It seemed obvious that secrecy was part of their plan. The soldiers turned at the corner of Port Street and Spates Lane, then turned again at Longview Heights. That was where Victor Bimm lived. Aldersan was severely troubled as the troops proceeded toward the regent's residence.

Aldersan was crouching behind a horseless wagon when the full ball of the sun popped over the horizon and sent the last shadows of night fleeing across the sky. To his dismay he watched as the soldiers gathered at the regent's front gate. A lead soldier approached the gate and rapped three times. He could hardly believe his eyes when the gate opened and the troops jogged freely into the compound. It appeared as if the regent's guard had been expecting the foreign troops.

Aldersan was just beginning to assess the import of what he was seeing when he heard someone move. Suddenly a pair of strong arms grabbed him roughly from behind. Before he was knocked unconscious, he turned and caught a glimpse of two men in drab-green uniforms.

Although each of us, as individuals, may entertain brave speculations in our daydreams, we never really know how we will respond to a life-threatening situation until we are tested by such an experience. It is one thing to slay a dragon in theory, and quite another to meet the beast in reality.

The truth is: Danger wears many different hats, and sometimes the only sane response is to look skyward and plead for divine intervention.

Aldersan Hale was not a philosopher or a religious type. He was an artist with a passion for the texture, weight, and shape of the things he could see in this world. Although he did believe that every object had an inner nature, he rarely thought of those things he could not touch or see. As a result, he had no opinion about whether or not there were intelligent powers in the hidden realms above. And yet Aldersan did have a human heart (which had a will of its own), and when he finished bouncing off the stone floor where the soldiers had tossed him, he looked up and cried, "Help."

Because of her interest in the Lydia Swain case, the angel Natalie had attuned herself to the sound of Aldersan Hale's voice. So now, when the poor fellow cried desperately for help, she was able to hear him loud and clear. She peered down into Korasan, located the frightened artist, quickly analyzed the situation, and flew off to find Ebol.

As the reader might guess, Ebol was snoozing when Natalie arrived at his cloud. Although the kick she planted on his rear was not meant to do harm, it was applied emphatically.

Ebol awoke with a start. "What the devil!"

Natalie smiled apologetically.

"Thanks, Natalie. That was pleasant," Ebol said sarcastically as he stood and rubbed his derriere.

Natalie wasted no time in coming to the point. "Ebol, are you intending to answer Lydia Swain's prayer?"

"You had to kick me awake to ask that?"

"Yes, as a matter of fact, I did," Natalie replied tersely. "It so happens that Aldersan Hale is in a pot of trouble, and if you are going to answer Lydia's prayer, I suggest you get started soon."

Ebol's frown lingered. "For what it's worth, Lydia Swain has changed the specifics of her prayer. Now she has a whole list of things she wants done."

Natalie was in no mood for excuses. "Be real, Ebol. We

are angels. It is not becoming of our kind to quibble over details. If you choose to shirk your duty, then do so . . . but don't look to me for sympathy. That girl called you, and you alone. She needs help."

Ebol was stung by Natalie's words. She was right, of course. In his heart of angel hearts, he knew he must quit procrastinating and go see Charlotte soon.

⇥ 12

Aldersan looked up with a kind of weary half-interest as the yellow rays of the descending sun poured through the window in the west wall of the room where he was imprisoned. It was a small window, set high in the wall, and except for a crack under the door, it was the only source of light in the stone chamber. During the early hours of his incarceration he had made several unsuccessful attempts to scale the wall and reach the opening. Now, after a full day of confinement, he was resigned to watching the window . . . waiting for his captors to make the next move.

Although Aldersan was hungry, thirsty, physically exhausted, and uncertain about his personal safety, his thoughts were not for himself. Instead, he was thinking about the larger situation in which he found himself. No one had spoken to him, before or after his capture, and he had only the ramblings of his imagination to provide an explanation. The only thing he knew for sure was that he had been tossed into a room—apparently in a warehouse near the docks—from which there appeared no likely means of escape. Two unknowns haunted him: Who were the men in drab-green uniforms? And what was their purpose in Valerton?

The light in the window had faded to a flat gray when Aldersan was startled by the clanking sound of a bolt sliding across the outside of the door. He jumped to his feet and stood against the opposite wall. The door swung open and four soldiers entered the room. The smallest of the four men carried a lantern, while the largest of the group held a leather whip. Aldersan gulped. Numerous small lead weights had been braided into the end of the whip. The soldiers stared coolly at Aldersan, yet did not speak or give any sign of their intentions.

A moment later Victor Bimm strolled into view. He cast a grim look at Aldersan, then began to chuckle with sinister amusement. "Sire Hale."

It was instantly clear to Aldersan that the regent was in cahoots with the foreign troops. Evidently the rumors were true; the greedy official was selling out the guild.

Aldersan felt rage rising in him like a storm. Part of his anger was as a citizen of Korasan, and part of it was personal. He had gone twice to the regent's residence to collect the balance of payment due on the commissioned griffin, and both times he had been told to return another day. Finally he had given up hope of ever being paid. And so now, as the regent stood smiling his smug smile, Aldersan felt a sudden urge to charge forth and pummel the man.

Victor Bimm, having recently been forced to make unexpected concessions in his deal with Felix Drump, was feeling especially power hungry. "I see you do not deign to greet your regent."

A variety of angry replies rolled across Aldersan's mind, but after a glance at the soldier with the whip, he chose to keep his words to himself.

"I'm disappointed in you, Sire Hale. Tell me, what would possess a gifted artist such as yourself to associate with those lawless rebels who dare to plot against my will?"

Aldersan bit his lower lip. Suddenly he recalled the secret meetings his father and other guild members had been attending. Unfortunately, his face revealed his thoughts.

The regent could see from Aldersan's reaction that he had touched a nerve. "Ah, you do know what I am talking about."

Aldersan crossed his arms and scowled.

Victor Bimm smiled at the soldier with the whip, then sneered at Aldersan. "I prefer you cooperate of your own will. Yet willingly or not, you are going to tell me what you know about the plot against me."

For the first time since the regent's arrival, Aldersan spoke: "I don't know anything about a plot against anyone, but even if I did, I would not tell you."

The regent shrugged, then signaled for the soldiers to act. Two of them stepped forward and ripped off Aldersan's shirt. A third bound Aldersan's hands with rope.

"Do you wish to reconsider?" asked the Regent.

"Traitor!" shouted Aldersan. An instant later he felt the first lash of the whip cut into his back. Again the regent asked if he had anything to say, and again Aldersan shouted, "Traitor!"

Aldersan groaned at the second stroke of the whip, yet he uttered no complaint. He was determined neither to cry out nor to ask for mercy. His silence infuriated the regent, who ordered the soldiers to continue. Soon blood trickled down Aldersan's back. Still he would not speak.

On the seventh stroke of the whip Aldersan recalled telling his parents not to worry about his whereabouts, that he would be working in his studio throughout his vacation. On the tenth stroke his thoughts flew to his studio and the waiting block of jeefwood. Eleven strokes, twelve . . . Lydia's face flashed across his mind just before he slipped into unconsciousness.

The angel Natalie was watching as Aldersan flopped over in a pool of blood. She was horrified. If it had been acceptable for one of her kind to throw a tantrum, she definitely would have had a fit. (So many atrocities occur daily on Earth that angels would be in a constant tizzy if they allowed themselves to be affected by every injustice they witnessed.) As it was, she focused healing vibrations in Aldersan's direction and threw intermittent glances at the Karmatic Stairway to see if Ebol was coming down. She wished he would hurry. It seemed he had been on the ninth level for an exceptionally long time.

When Ebol had entered the ninth level, he was nearly blinded by a brilliant golden light. A moment later the light diminished and he heard an all-encompassing voice utter his name. *Or was it a voice?* The sound resonated so deeply in his soul that it might have been made by some great cosmic amplifying instrument. When his eyes adjusted to the powerful illumination, he saw that he was standing before the mighty seraph Charlotte. A raiment of oscillating flames licked her from head to toe. *Ebol*, she either said or thought—he could not tell—and he dropped to his knees.

The domain of heaven is comprised of nine levels divided laterally into nine sectors. Watching over each of the sectors is one of the nine majestic seraphim. In the celestial hierarchy, seraphim hold the highest rank next to God. Below them reside the cherubim, the thrones, the dominions, the virtues, the powers, the principalities, the archangels, and, finally, the angels. Although some cherubs are occasionally allowed in the presence of the Almighty (usually in the capacity of cupbearers), only a seraph is able to withstand The Pure Light That Is The Maker Of All. Understanding this, the reader might imagine Ebol's awe as he looked upon the flame-licked Charlotte. (Had Ebol not been a soul who had once experienced the true feeling, his sheer proximity to the great being might have caused him to vanish.)

Of the nine majestic seraphim, Charlotte was the most stern. She kindly modulated her voice so that Ebol would not be entirely overwhelmed by its sound: "Why are you here?"

"I ah . . . came to-to-to . . ." stammered Ebol. He began to quake so severely that his words refused to depart from his mouth.

"To consult with me," Charlotte finished Ebol's line of thought. Being omniscient, she already knew everything.

"Yes. To consult," Ebol blurted. "I . . . well, you see, I've been awoken—I mean, called. I've been called."

It would be inaccurate to say that the great, flame-licked Charlotte actually laughed, but she did smile with such radiance that sparks flashed from her all-seeing eyes. "It must have been a clear voice that called you awake."

"Very clear." Ebol rose from his knees. He was gaining courage with each second spent in Charlotte's divine presence. "The voice was so clear, in fact, that I am almost certain the speaker has the potential for the true feeling."

Although Charlotte was able to discern all simply by looking at Ebol, she granted him the courtesy of showing interest in his case. "Please, tell me about the one who called you."

Ebol took a deep breath. "It's a girl, about sixteen. Her name is Lydia Swain. She lives in Korasan," he began. Then, as he presented his story, he grew so absorbed in telling it that he forgot where he was and began rubbing the spot on his bottom where Natalie had kicked him.

Mind yourself, Ebol. Charlotte's unspoken words blared in his head like the sounding of ten trumpets.

"Oops, excuse me." Ebol blushed from wingtip to wingtip.

The flames licking Charlotte turned from orange to red, and with a furrowing of her brow she stilled the words in Ebol's mind. She had heard all she wanted to hear. Ponderously, like a judge, she studied Ebol from head to toe. He quivered under her gaze, fearing she might smite him accidentally.

Finally the great seraph rendered her verdict. "Lydia

Swain has made an honest appeal for help. She is deserved of divine intervention. It was right of you to approach me with this matter."

Ebol heaved a sigh of relief. Feeling encouraged, he asked the question that had beguiled him since Lydia began her appeals. "Charlotte, I've been wondering: Why me? Why did Lydia call me and not some other?

Charlotte was amused. "That is part of the beautiful mystery, Ebol. Perhaps you will understand why after you have completed your mission."

"My mission?" Ebol gulped.

"Yes, Ebol, your mission. Don't you wish to help Lydia?"

"I suppose I do," Ebol mumbled weakly. Then he added, with a touch of enthusiasm, "Of course I wish to help her."

"Then that is your mission." Charlotte's tone was firm and unambiguous. "Help Lydia Swain resolve the conflict that threatens her world."

Ebol wanted to ask for details, but the severe look that had appeared on Charlotte's face persuaded him to keep silent.

Charlotte held Ebol in her powerful gaze until she was sure she had his complete attention. "It is a grave matter when an angel visits Earth. While you are there, you must not allow any human to learn that you hail from heaven. Many subtle forces will hang in the balance when you enter the mortal world. Maintaining that balance will be your responsibility. Do you understand?"

Ebol nodded affirmatively, although he had no idea of what forces would hang in what balance.

"Then so be it," Charlotte decreed. "You will go down as soon as night covers Korasan. Bernard will oversee your descent. You will wear the clothes you had on when you arrived in heaven. You will be able to speak the language of Korasan. The moment you touch ground, your wings will disappear. They will be restored upon your return to heaven. To do so, say Bernard's name three times and he will lift you up." After pausing to let her words sink in, Charlotte added, "Your mission is over the moment you return. You will not be given a second chance to finish what is undone. The balance will be as you leave it. Have I left anything unclear?"

Ebol's mind was so full of questions, he hardly knew what to ask first. "What exactly am I supposed to do down there?"

Charlotte answered with a slight tone of strained patience. "Assist Lydia Swain in her efforts to overcome the menace that threatens her world."

"But how?" Ebol was deeply perplexed.

"The opportunities will present themselves. It is for you to recognize them and respond appropriately."

"But what if there are no opportunities?"

All six of Charlotte's wings bristled. She clearly did not appreciate Ebol's lack of faith. "Arrangements will be made. You will be in the right place at the right time. It will be up to you to seize the opportunity when it comes."

Ebol was properly admonished. Who was he to question the word of Charlotte? He bowed humbly. "I will do my best."

"Now go." Charlotte pointed with a wing. "The angel

Natalie waits for you. She has news of recent developments in Korasan."

"Thank you for your gracious time," Ebol said as he turned to leave the ninth level. Then he hesitated and turned again. He had been hoping Charlotte would grant him some special power to employ during his mission. And now—well, here he was in her presence—wasn't this an opportunity?

But Charlotte read Ebol's mind and cut him off before he could formulate a request. "Special powers attract attention. Remember the balance. You are not to reveal your identity as an angel. Just trust, Ebol. You will succeed."

Again Ebol felt a pang of admonishment, and again he thanked Charlotte for her gracious time.

As he was departing, Charlotte called to him in a voice that was newly tender and sweet. "There is no need to thank me, Ebol. Just be grateful for the true feeling. It is the power that holds the balance together."

After sinking through a trapdoor of pain and drifting all day and part of the night in a dark void, Aldersan Hale awoke as the light of a first-quarter moon was shining through the window in the west wall. His stomach was stuck to the floor by a sheet of dried blood. It was late. The moon was on its way down.

For a long time he remained still, wondering why he—an artist who had no interest in politics—should find himself in the present situation.

Finally he lifted his head. Nearby was a flask of water, some bread, and a hunk of cheese. Soon he summoned the will to pry his stomach from the floor. His back rebelled against his every movement. Gritting his teeth to ward off the pain, he sat up and reached for the flask of water.

After eating, Aldersan made a pillow out of his torn shirt and placed it against the wall. He leaned a shoulder against the shirt. He was far from comfortable, of course, yet he did manage to mitigate the screaming edge of his pain.

The angel Natalie hovered above him, directing energy toward his mutilated back. Although the results of her ministrations fell short of what could fairly be called a miracle, she was able to accelerate the healing process to a remarkable degree. In a heavenly sort of way, she had turned sweet on the handsome young artist.

❧ 13

Though it was early in the morning as Lydia and Walter crossed the field between the cottage and the forest, she was already in a funk over the troubles besetting her, her family, and the Artisan Guild. The night before, Dale Hands, a guild member, had arrived at the cottage with a letter for her father and the other men. It was from Stuart Carver. Besides announcing that the harvest was to be postponed indefinitely, the letter contained the shocking news that Bash Landy had been ambushed and killed while transporting a wagonload of weapons purchased by the guild. From the marks on Bash's body and the damage done to the empty wagon, it appeared there had been a lengthy struggle. Bless his feisty soul, wrote Stuart. At least he went down fighting. The letter ended with a warning to be on the lookout for foreign soldiers wearing drab-green uniforms. No one was sure of the connection yet, but it was believed that the soldiers were responsible for Bash's demise. Lloyd, Malcomb, and Vassal had pestered Dale with questions before he departed, but Dale had just shrugged and said he knew no more than what Stuart had written.

By the measure of most individuals, Lydia was a rather independent person. Having grown up apart from other children, she had learned early in life to rely on herself first and on others later, if at all. Yet now things were different. Now she was faced with the overwhelming complications of a world gone wrong, and she felt an almost desperate need for someone with whom she might share her burdens. What she needed was a friend. She had her parents, of course, but as any teenager knows, that was not the same as having a friend.

If only Antoinette was here, she thought, the day would be so much easier to bear. If only I had someone other than Walter to speak with. (When Walter saw Lydia looking at him with such a sorrowful expression, he whimpered and hung his head. If only I were a bigger dog, he thought, she would probably be happy.)

Lydia stopped at the edge of the field before entering the shaded world of the Jeefwood Forest. *Strength* and *grace* were the words that came into her mind. Although she had walked into these woods at least a thousand times before, the giant trees never failed to impress her with their quiet and enduring power. It was as if they had been standing since the beginning of time and would continue standing for an eternity. She trembled at the thought that these wondrous plants might soon be gone.

Lydia had just reached the top of the lichen-covered boulder when she heard Walter growl nervously. He was staring at the base of a nearby tree, and whatever he saw there made his hair stand on end. "What is it, fellow?" she asked.

"*Grrr.*" Walter did not divert his attention from the tree.

Lydia climbed down from the boulder and went to see what was upsetting her dog. When she saw a pair of moccasins sticking out from behind the trunk of a jeef-wood, she froze. Maybe it was one of the foreign soldiers her father had warned her about. Whoever it was, his feet were not moving. Was he resting? Or dead? She shushed Walter with a whisper, then walked softly forward.

She did not know what to make of the young fellow sleeping under the jeefwood. Whoever he was, he sure was enjoying a deep snooze. He had on baggy pants, a loose shirt, and a rumpled jacket. All three items were the same sandy-brown color as his moccasins. She had never seen anyone like him. There was a reddish-copper tone to his skin, and he had curly brown hair arranged in an odd, bowl-like fashion.

He's too young to be a soldier, Lydia thought. He's probably a nomad from the Tajaki Plains. Suddenly she recalled the fortune-teller's words: *I see a sleeping stranger.*

101

Several minutes passed before curiosity finally got the better part of Lydia and she tossed a pebble at the stranger. It landed on his chest. The stranger's mouth fell open, his nose twitched, and then slowly he sat up. When he saw Lydia and Walter watching him, he smiled. "How do you do?"

It was an expression that Lydia had never heard before. "How do I do what?"

"You know—greetings. How are you?"

"Oh. I am fine," said Lydia. "How are you?"

The stranger hesitated a moment before replying, "Fine, I think. I think I'm fine." When Ebol attempted to stand, his legs began to wobble and he found it necessary to steady himself against the tree. Looking very unsure of himself, he mumbled, "Holy gamoly. The gravity here is pretty strong."

"Gravity?" said Lydia. "What's that?"

"You know, the stuff that holds you on the ground."

Lydia was not sure if the stranger was being serious or not. "Do you mean weight?"

"Yes, that's the stuff." The stranger nodded. He took a few tentative steps, then stopped and adjusted his stance. It felt odd not having wings attached to the back of his shoulders.

"Who are you?" Lydia asked in a polite yet very curious tone.

Natalie had prepared Ebol for just this sort of inquiry. "My name is Ebol. I'm an innocent vagabond who wanders the world. Don't worry, I'm friendly. What is your name?"

"Lydia. My father keeps these woods. I live in a cottage not far from here."

Ebol stifled a yawn. "Lydia. That's a nice name."

"Thank you. This is Walter."

Ebol nodded and Walter wagged his tail.

"Excuse me if I seem rude for saying this," said Lydia, "but I've never seen anyone who . . . who, I mean, where are you from?"

Natalie had prepared him for this question as well. "I am originally from Yegopt."

"Yegopt? Where in the world is that?"

"It's a long, long ways from here, Lydia. Way on the other side of the Hunderian Mountains," explained Ebol. Then he quickly changed the subject. "So, tell me, what's happening?"

"Happening?"

"You know, what is going on with you these days?"

"Oh," Lydia said glumly. "That will take a while to answer."

"Then take your time," Ebol countered cheerfully. "I've got plenty of time. Let's sit somewhere and I'll listen."

Lydia led Ebol to her boulder. As they were getting settled atop the big rock, Ebol glanced up and grinned for Natalie's benefit. Yet Natalie was not watching; she was busy sending healing vibrations into the warehouse where Aldersan Hale was imprisoned.

Somehow Aldersan had passed the night without losing his mind or his will to live. Now it was the next day, and though his back was still very sore, it pained him less than he had imagined it might. Earlier, one of the guards had rolled a breadfruit into the room. Aldersan ate this slowly, thoughtfully, with his brown eyes turned pensively toward the small window. He was wondering when the contemptible regent would return.

Sometime about noon Aldersan heard a commotion on the other side of the thick door. A moment later it opened and in stumbled Stuart Carver and Aldersan's father, Craig. They had been treated roughly. Both had blood dripping from their mouths and noses, and one of Stuart's eyes was puffed closed.

"Dad!" Aldersan stood and rushed to his father.

It took Craig Hale a moment to grasp the facts. "Aldersan! My lord, son. Are you all right?"

"I'm all right. I'll make it. But Dad, are you hurt badly?"

"Naw. Hardly at all," Craig lied. Although he and Aldersan liked and respected each other, they had never been exceptionally close. "Your mother is worried sick about you. She went twice to the studio to warn you that trouble was brewing."

Just then Stuart Carver hoisted himself off the floor and nodded to Aldersan. Even in the present circumstances, there was an aura of dignity and command that surrounded the man. "What are you doing here?"

"I'm not sure," Aldersan answered honestly. "I was out early yesterday morning, and I saw soldiers coming ashore from a boat in the harbor. It left as soon as the soldiers got off. Anyway, they seemed suspicious, so I followed them to the regent's residence. I was watching from behind a wagon when two of the soldiers jumped me."

Craig Hale suddenly noticed the wounds on Aldersan's

back. "Good lord! It looks like you've been whipped. Did the soldiers do that to you?"

"Yep." Aldersan nodded. "Victor Bimm was here yesterday. He wanted to know about the guild's plot against him. I didn't know what he was talking about."

"That man has gone too far." Craig swore heatedly. "The next time I see him, I'm going to crush his fat, oily head."

"He has gone too far," agreed Stuart. "And I suspect he now feels he has enough evidence to concoct charges of treason against the guild."

"What kind of evidence, Mr. Carver?" asked Aldersan.

Stuart frowned. "Some of his personal troops burst into my house about an hour ago. They caught your father and me with a rather incriminating letter to Sa Viddledass."

Lydia and Ebol had been sitting on the boulder for several hours when it dawned on Lydia that she had been talking almost the whole time. There was a strangely reassuring quality about her new acquaintance that seemed to draw the words right out of her. She had told him about the fortune-teller, about Aldersan, and about the guild's trouble with the regent. Perhaps it was the luster in his brown eyes that inspired her to talk—they reminded her of the fortune-teller's eyes—or perhaps it was simply because Ebol was there to listen. And now, as she pondered her own loquacity, she was struck by the notion that Ebol had seemed to understand and anticipate many of her feelings. "I'm sorry," she said with a blush. "I've been rambling on like a river."

"Don't apologize to me, Lydia. I'm truly fascinated. I find other people's lives interesting."

"Thanks for saying so, but my life isn't interesting at all. I'm just a boring person with a boring life."

"You're not boring," Ebol said with a kind smile. He had discovered that he was rather fond of Lydia in person. "You lead a quiet life, that's all. Besides, interesting is a concept based on appreciation, and different people appreciate different things. Like me. I appreciate you."

"Hmmm."

"Anyway, things could change soon and get more interesting than you ever imagined."

Lydia shrugged. "Maybe they're changing already. Just this morning I was thinking how much I needed a friend to talk to. And . . . well, here you are."

"Everyone needs friends," Ebol noted philosophically. "Now, let's hear more about this artist you met at the spring dance. From what you've told me, he sounds interesting."

"Oh, he is," Lydia sighed. "Or at least he was . . . as far as I could tell. To be honest, I'm not sure if Aldersan remembers me."

"I bet he does."

Lydia sighed again, and then, in a dreamy manner, she began to discuss those thoughts nearest to her heart.

ᐱ14

At the end of the day, when Lydia tried to persuade Ebol to join her at the cottage for supper, he declined. "You go right ahead. I've had quite a journey. I think I'll just bed down under that tree for the night."

"But aren't you hungry?" asked Lydia. "I know I am, and I had breakfast. You haven't eaten all day."

"People eat more than is necessary," Ebol replied evasively. The fact was, he would not be requiring food during his earthly visit.

"But they do eat," Lydia noted.

When Ebol saw the look of scrutiny on Lydia's face, he knew he must say something to divert her curiosity. "Don't worry about me. I have a little manna in my jacket."

"Manna? What's that?"

Ebol blushed. He was not doing a very good job at being discreet. "It's . . . well it's a flat cake that is a favorite with us vagabonds. I wouldn't say it's very tasty, but a small bit goes a long ways."

"Oh." Lydia nodded. She supposed it was only natural that vagabonds would have peculiar diets. "In the morning I'll bring you some real food."

"Yes, tomorrow." Ebol yawned. He was quite eager for some gravity-bound sleep. "So, you and Walter go on home, and I'll see you in the morning. Maybe by then I will have thought of a way to answer your . . . I mean, resolve your dilemmas."

That night, after supper, Lydia sat quietly by the kitchen door and listened to the men talk about what a brave and decent man Bash Landy had been. Perhaps it was a good thing, they said, that he had never married. They expressed many regrets that none of them would be there for the funeral. Afterward they speculated on what might or might not happen during the upcoming weeks. Lloyd and Malcomb shared similarly dim outlooks, although each sketched radically different scenarios. Only Vassal was in the least bit optimistic. (The men did not yet know that Aldersan Hale, Craig Hale, and Stuart Carver had been arrested.)

Later, Glenda stepped out on the porch and signaled for Lydia to come inside. Reluctantly, Lydia got up and went into the kitchen. At first she considered telling her mother about the traveler from Yegopt who was sleeping in the forest. Then she decided that before saying anything, she would wait and see if Ebol was still there in the morning. One could never be too sure about a vagabond.

The next morning, after a hearty breakfast with her parents and their guests, Lydia was spreading butter on a roll to take to Ebol when her father's ears picked up a distant sound. "Everyone *shhh*," Lloyd whispered. "Someone is coming."

A moment later everyone else heard the rhythmic pounding of a horse in full gallop. They all remained silent as it grew closer; then Vassal snickered and Lloyd moaned as the rhythm was interrupted by an aggressive honking sound, followed by a shout. Weezie had obviously attacked the horse and rider.

Everyone bolted outside. It was Dale Hands again, riding a different horse than before. He reined the creature to a halt by the cottage fence and waited until Lydia was able to restrain the persnickety goose. Dale was looking exceedingly worse for the wear. Yet concern for his physical state was forgotten as soon as he had a chance to relay the news that had prompted him to return so quickly from Valerton. "Yesterday the mercenaries working for Bimm arrested Stuart Carver and Craig Hale. They're in one of the regent's empty warehouses," said Dale, huffing for breath. He paused long enough to drink from the glass of water Glenda gave him, then continued with a rush of words: "We think they have someone else in there too. Last night Tubby Chance saw a soldier enter with three meals. It might be Craig Hale's son, Aldersan. He's been missing for a couple of days."

Lydia was kneeling in the yard, holding Weezie, when Aldersan's name was mentioned. A sinking feeling in her heart made her weak for an instant, and the feisty goose almost broke free.

An intense twenty-minute debate ensued, and when it was over, Dale, Malcomb, and Vassal mounted their respective horses and rode off to see what they could achieve in Valerton. Lloyd had reluctantly agreed that he and his family would be safer if they moved to the village. So, while the departing men were still in sight, he instructed his family to prepare to follow.

"You have two hours to get ready," Lloyd said to Lydia. "You and your mother will stay at the Bells'. Pack appropriately. We might be gone for some time."

"Okay, Dad, but what about Walter?"

"Better take him with you."

"And Weezie?" Lydia asked before she really thought about the matter.

It was Glenda who answered the question. "Weezie can fend for herself. She'll have the sheep and the cows to keep her company. I'll put plenty of food in the barn for all of them."

Lydia was frantic as she ran to her room and pulled her traveling case out from under the bed. So many thoughts flashed through her mind, she could not concentrate: Was Aldersan in that warehouse with the others? Was he okay? What was her father going to do? Would he also be arrested? I must water my jeeflets before we go. Antoinette—I'll be seeing her tonight. That's good. Now, what should I take to wear? Suddenly she remembered that Ebol was waiting in the forest. She hesitated for just a moment, then leapt from her bedroom window and started running.

As Lydia hurried toward the grove, it occurred to her that Ebol may have already risen and departed. But when she arrived at the jeefwood tree where she had left him, she was glad to find him still sleeping.

"Ebol," she called. When the sleeper failed to stir, she repeated the name at a higher volume. Again there was no response. Under normal circumstances Lydia would have exercised a fair amount of patience, but just now she was compelled by the urgency of the day's events. She stepped forward, and with a pointed foot she gently poked Ebol's backside.

"Holy gamoly, Natalie!" Ebol sat upright and looked around. Then he realized where he was. "Oh, good morning, Lydia. For a second I thought you were someone else."

"Sorry to wake you like that, but I'm in a terrible hurry. The regent has arrested the president of the Artisan Guild, and I have to go to Valerton with my parents."

"What?" Ebol rubbed the sleep from his eyes.

"Dale Hands said maybe Aldersan Hale is in prison too."

"Slow down, Lydia. Who is Dale Hands?"

"Dale is a guild member. He has ridden back and forth from Valerton twice in the past two days."

"Hmmm." Ebol stood and rubbed debris from his back. "What is this about Aldersan Hale in prison?"

"I don't know for sure," Lydia blurted. "Dale just said he was missing. I don't know what to think. At the moment it seems like the whole world has gone mad."

Ebol pursed his lips thoughtfully. Although he knew that Aldersan was locked in the warehouse, he did not like to see Lydia in such an anxious state. "You said Aldersan was an artist. If he is missing, maybe he is just out wandering around somewhere with his head in he clouds. Artists do that sort of thing all the time. I wouldn't worry about him."

"It's possible." Lydia sighed. Then suddenly she remembered the buttered roll sitting on the kitchen table. "Oops. I forgot to bring you breakfast."

"That's okay. When do you go to Valerton?"

111

"Soon. First I have to go back and finish packing. Then I need to take care of my plants. I just wanted to come and tell you I was leaving."

"Thanks for letting me know," Ebol mumbled. "I guess I'll see you there."

"You're going to Valerton!" Lydia exclaimed. "Why don't you come with us? The road might be dangerous now because of the problems with soldiers and everything."

Ebol pursed his lips in thought again, then shrugged. "No. You go on without me, Lydia. I'll find you there."

"I hope you will. I'll be staying with my cousin Antoinette Bell. Her house is on Lumber Lane. It's a block north of Guild Avenue."

"Bell, huh?"

"That's right. Antoinette Bell. Just ask anyone for directions. Her father's name is Willard."

"Sounds simple enough," Ebol allowed. "I'll see you there."

"Great. So, I better go now," said Lydia, but before racing away, she extended her hand and added, "You know Ebol, I don't have many friends. I want you to know that I sincerely enjoyed talking with you yesterday."

"It was my pleasure." Ebol blushed as he clasped Lydia's hand and shook it up and down.

After running about fifty yards through the Jeefwood Forest, Lydia stopped and called, "Please, try to find me."

"I'll find you," Ebol replied with a shout.

"And be careful on the road," Lydia added. "No one

knows where those soldiers are, or what they might be up to."

"I'll be careful," Ebol hollered. He felt just great. Here he was on Earth again, this time with a mission, and friend who cared about his well-being.

❧ 15

It was four days before first-summer when Ebol set out along the old wooded lane toward Valerton. He could see fresh tracks from where the Swains had gone ahead. His pace was leisurely, and as he walked he derived great pleasure from the simple knowledge that he was back again on terra firma. The experience was proving to be quite a joy; on this fine, sunshiny day near first-summer in Korasan, heaven seemed almost drab by comparison. Frequently he stopped to admire a view, appreciate a birdsong, or sniff a wafting scent.

Later, when night fell over the lane, Ebol ambled into the woods, spread his jacket upon a patch of clear ground, and made himself comfortable. He had never been very picky about where he slept, as long as he found the chance to do so.

About the same time Ebol began to snore, the door to a heavily guarded room in a warehouse in Valerton swung open and Victor Bimm sauntered inside. He was welcomed by a snarl, a sneer, and a grunt. Prudently the regent had not entered alone. Encircling him were seven sturdy soldiers. One carried a lantern; the other six were armed with truncheons or swords.

The regent greeted his captives with a mocking air of overt friendliness. "Good evening, gentlemen. Anyone care for a game of tiddledywinks?"

Stuart Carver made another grunting noise. He was in no mood for nonsense. He challenged the regent with bold disregard for his own safety. "Bimm, you have no right to hold us prisoners. And what you have done to this man"—Stuart turned to Aldersan—"is nothing less than a cowardly crime."

Victor Bimm glanced at Aldersan before replying to Stuart in an almost repentent tone. "I regret that I was prompted to such an extreme action, but illegal weapons were being smuggled into Valerton, and as the ruler here, it was my duty to use whatever means necessary to learn why those weapons were purchased in the first place."

"You tortured an innocent man," Stuart shouted angrily.

The regent's smooth, diplomatic facade began to dissipate. "Calm down, Carver. I am here to make you a reasonable offer."

No longer able to control his rage, Craig Hale lurched at the heavyset regent. "I'm going to crush your oily head."

Craig was immediately conked on the head with a truncheon. He sank to the floor with a groan. Aldersan was about to rush to his father's aid, but Craig stayed his son with a raised hand. He was wobbly and woozy, but he was okay.

Victor Bimm shrugged as if to say the consequences of Craig's action were not his fault. "Let's not bandy about here, Carver. We both know what this is all about."

"Yes, we both know," Stuart retorted. "It's about one man's greed."

Victor Bimm frowned. "This has nothing to do with greed. It is about the people, and about improving the economy of Valerton. Jeefwood, of course, is the key to doing that. Logically, I am turning that key."

Although Stuart trembled with anger, he managed to keep his voice steady. "The crafting of jeefwood is a tradition in Korasan that goes back hundreds of years. The products of the guild are world renowned. Making those products provides a way of life for many people. In that sense, you are correct—this is about people. But if you allow jeefwood to be sold on the open market, that way of life will disappear. What will the people do then?"

"They will be richer," replied the regent. "My plan calls for a part of the profits to be distributed among the populace. Of course, the men who harvest the trees will receive a larger percentage that the others. That's where the guild comes in."

"Your plan calls for you to get rich on the backs of others," Stuart countered. "Your greed will not be tolerated."

"Carver, I used to think you were an intelligent man . . . but obviously I was wrong. The irony here is that you're the greedy one. You just want to keep the jeefwood for yourself and your greedy supporters. This village could be rich."

"We are prosperous already. What you propose will bring about the destruction of a forest that has stood since before Korasan's noble ancestors ever dreamed of coming here."

Victor Bimm now knew that the guild would oppose him no matter what he said. "Save your fancy talk, Carver. It's about as eloquent as the letter you wrote to Sa Viddledass. And it's going to do you the same amount of good, which is none."

"Eventually the sovereign will hear of what you've done."

"Indeed, he will hear," the regent agreed with a sinister chuckle. "I have written to Sa Viddledass and explained how I am acting in accordance with the wants of the populace."

Craig Hale, now partially recovered from the blow to his head, pointed an accusing finger at the regent. "Bash Landy was one of the populace. It will be in accordance with his will that I one day crush your head."

Victor Bimm ignored Craig and turned to Stuart. "You have a week. If you refuse to cooperate at the end of that time, I will hire independents to cut my timber."

"Good luck," snapped Stuart. "Jeefwoods don't fall as easily as your integrity . . . if you ever had any to begin with."

Ebol meandered into Valerton's central square the following afternoon. Although his mission had hardly just begun, he was already beginning to worry about his ability to be in the right place at the right time. To begin with, he could not remember how to find Lydia. Had she said she would be staying on Annie Lane off Bell Avenue? Or was it Lumber North on Guild Street? And what was the cousin's name? He wished now that he had paid closer attention.

Ebol's feet were sore (he had not walked on solid ground for two centuries), and so he found a sunny spot on the courthouse steps and sat down to rest. As he watched the square, he grew increasingly fascinated by the ebb and flow of humanity passing before his eyes. Some went in straight lines, while others followed zigzag lines on round-about routes. Some seemed to know where they were going and why, while others appeared nebulous and uncertain. Some walked stiffly, some strode with arms swinging, and some just drifted from spot to spot. This is life, he thought. Each to his own, at his own pace. He had almost forgotten how individualistic mortal beings could be. Each face read like a different book, telling an original story filled with personalized victories and disappointments.

After philosophizing for about twenty minutes, Ebol suddenly recalled that he was on a mission . . . and that it wasn't going too well. He needed to find Lydia before any subtle forces had a chance to get out of whack.

He was soon distracted from his ruminations by the sound of a barking dog. It was Walter, and with him, of course, was Lydia. "Ebol? Is that you?"

"Yes. Hello. Of course it's me," he answered gleefully.

Lydia and a dark-haired girl rushed to join the vagabond from Yegopt. "Ebol, this is my cousin Antoinette," said Lydia. "Antoinette, this is Ebol, the vagabond I told you about."

Antoinette grinned playfully. "The sleeping stranger. Such a pleasure to meet you."

"The pleasure is mine." Ebol bowed respectfully.

"Ebol, where did you get those clothes?" Antoinette could not restrain her curiosity. "I've never seen anything like 'em."

Ebol glanced down and blushed. "In Yegopt. My uncle made them. I guess they are out of fashion here."

Antoinette saw that she had embarrassed Ebol, and she did her best to make amends. "They do mark you as a foreigner, but they look durable, and I like that."

Now it was Ebol's turn to grin. "Durable they are. In fact, I doubt you'd believe me if I told you how long I've had them."

"You look fine," said Lydia as she sat down beside Ebol. "Gosh, I'm so glad we found you."

"Me too," Ebol adjoined sincerely. "And how are things with the guild and the regent? Has the situation improved any?"

"No," Lydia said sadly. "The situation has gotten worse."

Antoinette suddenly raised a hand overhead and called out across the square. "Edbert. Here. Over here." (During the past few weeks her opinion of Edbert had changed for the better. As a result Antoinette had become less difficult to please.)

As Edbert approached, it was obvious that something was bothering him. "Hello," he greeted the group in a grave manner.

Antoinette introduced the two boys, then asked Edbert, "What is with the long face?"

Edbert directed his reply to Lydia. "I'm sorry to tell you this, but about an hour ago the regent's soldiers caught your father and three other men trying to help the prisoners escape."

Lydia shuddered. She was speechless. Walter, sensing his mistress's mood, began to whimper.

"What happened?" asked Antoinette.

Edbert fidgeted awkwardly. Obviously he was not comfortable being the bearer of bad news. "From what I heard, Mr. Swain had a bow and arrow, and he was trying to shoot rope through a window in the warehouse. And, well . . . the soldiers caught him."

"What happened to my dad?" Lydia asked in a cracking voice.

Edbert hesitated, reluctant to answer.

"Tell us," Antoinette ordered.

"Mr. Swain and the men with him were thrown in the warehouse with the other prisoners. Supposedly there was a pretty nasty fight before reinforcements got there."

Lydia struggled to hold back her tears. "I better go home. Mom might need me. Ebol . . . I'm not sure where to tell you to go."

"Don't worry about me," said Ebol. "I'll be fine."

As Antoinette prepared to leave with Lydia and Walter, she suggested to Edbert, "Maybe you could take care of Ebol. He's a vagabond. He probably needs a place to stay or something."

"Yes, dear." Edbert sighed wearily.

A moment later Antoinette turned and called across the square, "Edbert, since Ebol is a guest, and since you have such a huge wardrobe, maybe you could lend him an outfit."

During the next several hours Edbert was a solicitous and informative host as he led Ebol on a walking tour of Valerton. It was an old village, settled by sailors some four hundred years before. There were many handsome sights to see, and as they went from place to place, Edbert (limited only by his vocabulary and his imagination) did his best to imbue each sight with a rich and exciting heritage. Although Ebol soon grew weary from all the walking, he listened courteously to all he was told and even asked an occasional question. Of all the things he saw, the guild building on the south side of the square piqued his interest most. It was made of massive jeefwood timbers and it towered over the neighboring buildings.

"The Artisan Guild is very important in Korasan," Edbert explained. "It has been for the last century. Even before there was a guild, there was a group of families that made things out of jeefwood to trade with the nomads. The guild protects the tradition."

"Sounds like a good tradition," Ebol observed.

"It's good," Edbert agreed sullenly. "I just hope it lasts. There's a rumor that the regent wants to do away with the guild."

"Can't someone stop him?"

"Maybe. Maybe not. Again, it's just a rumor, but the

word is that the women in Valerton are going to demon-strate tomorrow. But don't tell anyone—they don't want the regent finding out until after they're organized."

That evening Edbert offered to treat Ebol to a meal in a favorite local restaurant. When Ebol politely declined, Edbert insisted. So Ebol declined again, and again Edbert insisted. The issue was finally resolved when Ebol allowed Edbert to buy him a bread roll and a hunk of cheese. Ebol placed the offering in a jacket pocket.

Later, as they were sitting in the square, Ebol yawned and asked Edbert if he knew of a place where he could bed down for the night. Edbert considered for a moment, then said that he knew just the place.

Soon the boys were standing in front of a building with a sign that read SEEDS. To the left of the sign was a door. It was unlocked. Edbert opened the door and explained, "My father owns the building. There's an attic up those steps where an artist has a studio, but I don't think he's going to be using the place anytime soon."

"Are you sure it's all right?"

"It's fine. The seed shop closed hours ago."

"I mean, are you sure it's all right with the artist?" Ebol had viewed this building from heaven, and he recognized it as the place where he had seen Aldersan Hale.

"Shouldn't think he'd mind." Edbert seemed surprised by the question. "An artist is an artist, and everyone knows artists are open-minded."

Ebol acquiesced with a shrug. The past two days of gravity-bound existence had put him in the mood for some serious snoozing.

"I'll come fetch you in the morning. Then maybe we can go see if Antoinette or Lydia needs anything."

"Fine," Ebol agreed with a yawn.

A moment later his jacket was in a heap on the floor and he was stretched out on Aldersan's workbench. He had hardly begun to snore when a pair of lucky mice found the bread and cheese in the jacket pocket.

Late that night, as Valerton slept—some against stone walls, some in soft featherbeds, some on wooden workbenches—the angel Natalie watched over one and all. The vibrations she had been emanating had done wonders for Aldersan's back, as well as diminished the bruises on Dale, Lloyd, Malcomb, and Vassal. Even so, she was frustrated that she could not do more to help the regent's victims. She knew mortals usually reaped what they sowed and that the regent would probably get his due, but the knowledge did little to ease her frustration. She also knew that some things took a long time to come full circle.

Time. That maestro of maestros. Even though angels have an eternal supply of the stuff, they can do nothing about its rate of passing. Even an angel can dance no faster than the music plays.

ᕗ16

Ebol was awakened soon after dawn by a shaft of sunlight streaming through a crack in the studio wall. When he blinked open his eyes, his attention was drawn to Aldersan's unfinished sculpture. He had not noticed it in the darkness of the night, but now the carving dominated the space and captured the full focus of his waking mind.

Ebol studied the block of jeefwood with an admiring eye. He could see from his perspective that a woman was in the process of taking shape. These simple, innocent mortals, he thought. They are eternally fascinated with the human form.

An hour later, when Edbert entered the studio with a package under his arms, Ebol was still horizontal on the workbench. "Good morning," Edbert chirped. "I brought you some duds." Then he threw a cursory glance at the unfinished sculpture and remarked, "You know, that looks a lot like Lydia."

Ebol sat up and studied the sculpture anew. Edbert was right; it did resemble Lydia. It seemed odd to Ebol that he had not noticed before. Perhaps humans were not so simple and innocent after all.

Edbert dropped the package he was carrying in a chair.

"I'll wait for you outside. Be quick about getting dressed. There's going to be a protest."

"A protest?"

"Yep. The women and children from the guild families are organizing a march down to the regent's warehouse. They're going to demand that the prisoners be set free."

"Women and children. Are we going?"

"Yeah, but we'll stay in the background," Edbert said as he turned to descend the rickety stairs. "I mean, heck, we're both men, more or less."

Ebol did not reply. Instead he moved to inspect the contents of the package that Edbert had left for him. He was in for a bit of a shock.

Edbert and Ebol arrived in the square while the protesters were still amassing. A few dark clouds had gathered in the east, adding an ominous note to the gathering. About a half-dozen women carried signs calling for the release of the unjustly jailed guild members. Others toted wicker baskets filled with food.

The mayor, Louise Spate, stood on a box at the center of the square. Her presence was like a magnet. Congregating around her were grandmothers, aunts, mothers, wives, sisters, and children of every description. All told, nearly eighty people had gathered to hear the mayor.

Not all of Valerton's female citizenry or its youth had turned out for the protest. Most of those who stayed away were generally sympathetic to the guild, yet for various reasons they were reluctant to get involved. Some had jobs to keep them away, others were afraid of jeopardizing economic ties to the regent—either direct or indirect— and many remained at home simply because they were apathetic. Every society in the world is plagued to some degree by political apathy. Korasan was no exception.

After declaring that he had something to do and would return soon, Edbert left Ebol standing alone at the edge of the square. In the distance Ebol could see Lydia speaking with a woman who appeared to be her mother. She was. As Ebol watched the pair—both were obviously deeply troubled by the situation—it occurred to him that since his arrival on Earth he had napped, chatted, and done a great deal of walking, yet he had achieved nothing toward the success of his mission. Suddenly he felt rather worthless. And adding insult to his shame, he also felt utterly ridiculous in the checkered pants and bright yellow shirt that Edbert had lent him.

Lydia did a double take when she saw Ebol standing awkwardly at the side of the square. He was holding his jacket in front of him as if he was trying to hide behind the garment, and a look of intense embarrassment colored his face.

Lydia, looking rather grim herself, went to greet Ebol. "Hi. I guess you heard we are going to protest."

"Edbert told me," Ebol said with a nod. Hearing Lydia's troubled voice heightened his feelings of ineptitude.

"I don't know if demonstrating will help or not." Lydia frowned pessimistically.

"It might help," Ebol allowed with shrug. "At least your father and the other men in the warehouse will know someone is trying to help them."

"That's something, I guess." Lydia sounded as if she was about to cry. "You know, Ebol, you don't have to march with us. This is a local problem. It might be . . . well, with you being a foreigner and all, it might be dangerous for you."

Ebol was moved by Lydia's concern. Considering all that was on the line for her and her family, he saw it as a testament to her good character that she should think of his welfare at a time like this. It was another clear sign that she was a vessel of the true feeling. He was tempted to tell her that he had already been rewarded an eternal life, and that (in theory, at least) danger meant nothing to him. Instead he said, "I'd like to march with you, Lydia. You confided in me yesterday, and that made me feel trusted. To a vagabond, there is no better feeling than being trusted by a stranger. I want to help any way I can."

"That's awful good of you," Lydia gushed, then stepped forward to kiss Ebol on the cheek.

Ebol reddened and looked shyly at his feet. No one outside of his family had ever kissed him before. What, he wondered, did etiquette call for him to do? Was he supposed to smile and say thank you? Should he kiss her back? (The angel Natalie was watching as Ebol stared bashfully at the ground. She knew it was a serious moment for her celestial cohort, and yet she could not restrain from laughing. In all her years of existence, she had never seen anyone more comically attired.)

Much to Ebol's relief, Louise Spate chose that moment to begin speaking and Lydia turned to hurry across the square. He followed, and together they joined Antoinette at the back of the crowd.

Louise Spate's plan was simple and straightforward. The protesters were to march in an orderly fashion down Guild Avenue, turn right on Port Street, and approach the regent's warehouse in clear view of the soldiers. After reaching their destination, everyone was to assemble peacefully in the street opposite the guarded entrance.

As the mayor was cautioning for everyone to remain calm, no matter what happened, Edbert Sands appeared at Antoinette's side. He was short of breath. He carried a placard that said LIBERATE THE ARTISANS. He handed it to Antoinette and whispered, "Dad said I have to stay neutral or he will disown me, but I made this in case you'd like to carry it."

Antoinette knew that Edbert's father was an important businessman who stood to lose a lot from offending the regent. She also knew that Mr. Sands was a strict disciplinarian. Even so, she gave Edbert a reproachful look. "Okay, I'll carry it. Just remember, you owe me."

"I owe you? For what?"

Antoinette frowned and shook her head. "For standing up to those bullies on your behalf."

Edbert thought, but did not say: *Girls—if only they weren't so cute.*

The soldiers from Zapin who guarded the stone building were a stoic lot. To the man, they stood stone-faced and silent. Some had longbows slung over their shoulders, others had swords in sheaths at their sides, a few held wooden truncheons, and one particularly wicked-looking individual had a leather whip draped over his chest. All told, twenty soldiers were spread out around the perimeter of the warehouse. Evidently the regent had learned of the protest and doubled up on security. The remainder of his troops were resting, or guarding his residence.

Ebol stayed close to Lydia as the protesters gathered quietly in the street opposite the warehouse entrance. Although he had no idea what was going to happen next, he sensed that this was one of the opportunities Charlotte had predicted.

Out of the corner of his eye Ebol saw Lydia peering skyward and moving her lips in silent prayer. *I'm here*, he wanted to tell her, *not there*. But of course he held his tongue: The balance must be maintained.

Louise Spate crossed the street to speak with a soldier wearing epaulets on his uniform. Although none of the protesters could hear what she said to the man, they could see from the shake of his head that he was opposed to whatever she had asked. An angry murmur arose from the throng, then grew into a chorus of strident shouts. Soon Violet Pender began to chant: "Down with Bimm. Free our men." Her words were quickly adopted by the others. "Down with Bimm. Free our men."

As the chanting grew louder, the protesters drew courage from their union and began to move toward the warehouse entrance. The soldiers tensed and readied their weapons. Still the women and children surged forward. A clash seemed inevitable and imminent, but then the agitated mob was abruptly distracted by the thunderous approach of soldiers on horseback. A traveling coach pulled by four muscular stallions trailed closely behind the riders.

The women and children cleared the street and ceased from their chanting. The coach halted between the protesters and the warehouse. A window opened and Victor Bimm's pointed pompadour appeared. It was followed by his wide face. His eyes searched for the mayor, who happened to be standing beside Lydia and Ebol. "Louise. What is your purpose in all this?"

Louise Spate retorted with a huff. "What is your purpose in jailing innocent men without charges?"

The regent smirked. He did not have much respect for the mayor. "Those men may not be as innocent as you imply. They are being held while an investigation is conducted into certain planned acts of rebellion against the sovereign."

"You know that isn't the truth," Louise said angrily.

Victor Bimm's steely gray eyes flickered with annoyance. "It's my duty to protect the general welfare of Valerton. If I determine that certain troublemakers need detaining, then that is the truth. And that is what will be done."

"Just how long do you intend to hold the men?" inquired Louise. "They have families to care for."

"For as long as I wish," the regent stated flatly.

Louise realized that Victor Bimm was not going to release the prisoners on this day, and so she attempted to wrest a lesser concession from the tyrant. "Many of the women have brought food for the prisoners. The least you can do is allow the food to be delivered."

After an exasperated roll of his eyes, Victor Bimm signaled to the soldier with the epaulets. The officer snapped to attention by the open window, and the regent instructed, "Collect all the baskets and check them for weapons. Then pick a couple of kids and permit them into the warehouse with the food. Allow them to visit for a short while."

"Yes, sir." The soldier saluted. "Just any kids?"

Sighing, as if the task was below his dignity, the regent pointed at Lydia and Ebol. "Those two: the girl with the fair hair and that clown in the checkered pants." Then Victor Bimm signaled to the coach driver, and the stallions lunged forward.

Ebol grimaced and glanced upward. Clearly the regent's choice had not been made by chance.

⊰⊱ 17

A s the food baskets were being collected, searched, and consolidated into two burlap sacks, Glenda Swain pulled Lydia aside and advised her, "You must keep your spirits up, dear. The men have enough to worry about without seeing a frightened face."

"Yes, Mom."

"Remind Lloyd that time is his friend when he whistles."

"Yes, Mom."

Then, as a soldier approached and signaled for Lydia

and Ebol to follow him, Glenda added in a whisper, "Ask your father if there is anything we might do to help."

"You will be allowed twenty minutes," the soldier said as he handed a sack to Lydia and a sack to Ebol.

The first thing Lydia noticed when she stepped into the dimly lit warehouse was the stench of men confined in a room without a toilet. The first thing Ebol noticed was the strained expressions on the prisoners' faces. He still had no idea why he, in particular, had heard Lydia's prayers and been called to Earth, yet he knew that his entrance into the warehouse was an opportunity for him to accomplish some aspect of his mission.

Lloyd cried out when he recognized his daughter. "Lydia! My sweet, sweet Lydia!"

"Dad!" Lydia dropped her sack and rushed into her father's open arms. While they were hugging, she peeked over his shoulder and saw Aldersan Hale. She was pleased by the look of recognition and surprise that sprang into Aldersan's eyes.

Ebol approached the other prisoners and set his sack on the floor. When Vassal Pender saw what was inside, he threw back his head and chortled, "Gifts from heaven!"

"What's this?" asked Malcomb Belt.

Ebol explained how the food had been collected from the protestors, and how he and Lydia had been chosen to deliver the offerings.

"Thanks. It was good of you to accept the appointment," said Vassal. He added in a curious tone, "I don't believe I've seen you in the village before."

"No, you haven't," Ebol admitted. "I'm from Yegopt."

"Yegopt?" Stuart Carver turned and examined Ebol with pointed interest. It seemed as if he was trying to remember some fact that he could not quite recall. After a moment he remarked with a shrug, "Yegopt is a long ways from Korasan."

"Yes, sir. I know. I'm a vagabond."

"What's you name?"

"Ebol."

"Ebol. Pleased to meet you. I'm Stuart. And that's Vassal. Malcomb. Dale. Craig, and Craig's son, Aldersan."

Ebol acknowledged each person with a nod and then stepped back from the group as Lloyd and Lydia approached. Lloyd said hello to Ebol before emptying the contents of the second sack onto the floor. The hungry men sat down and began to eat.

Stuart Carver was reaching for a boiled egg when he suddenly recalled what he had been trying to remember earlier. He left the egg where it lay and turned to Ebol. "You may be pleased to hear that Korasan's sovereign, Sa Viddledass, has a special affection for Yegoptians."

"He does?"

"Yes." Stuart smiled at the astonished youngster and explained. "Sa Viddledass is from an ancient line of Farroupe noblemen, but one of his distant forefathers was born in Yegopt. Legend has it that the mother of the sovereign's ancestor was traveling in Yegopt when the country was invaded by enemies. Her husband was killed. She was a passenger on a ship that sank somewhere off the coast. She too would have died if not for a young Yegop-

132

tian boy who sacrificed his life to save the woman. Soon after she was rescued from the sea she gave birth to a son. Since then, each generation of the Farroupe line has been taught to respect Yegoptians and to honor the nameless hero who sacrificed his life."

To say that Stuart's story struck home with Ebol would be a major understatement. Though he could hardly fathom the fact, he knew that he was the nameless hero of the story. In his head he could clearly hear the voice of the beautiful woman with the cobalt-blue eyes: *May God bless you, my savior. Your goodness will be remembered for centuries to come.*

While Ebol stood back from the group in humble awe of his own fate, Lydia sat beside her father, reeling with distraction. Not ten feet away from her sat the subject of her recent thoughts and prayers. And not only was Aldersan Hale sitting across from Lydia, he was watching her with decided interest. Of course, given Lydia's modest nature, she did not speak directly to Aldersan. However, her heart did jump up and down and shout.

Aldersan Hale was also reeling. Not ten feet away was the inspiration and model for his first life-sized sculpture. And she, in her own inimitable way, was beautiful. Until this moment he had thought of her purely as a model—as an image to work from—but now he suddenly became aware of feelings in himself that went beyond the call of his art.

Aldersan suppressed the urge to speak with Lydia. He did not wish to embarrass her or himself by speaking of personal matters in front of the other men.

The warehouse door opened and a soldier appeared. From behind him in the street came the sound of the protestors. They had taken up a new chant: *"We are the people. We are the song. We are the truth that stands against wrong."* The soldier pointed at Lydia and Ebol. "You have one minute. Then you must leave."

As the group was rising to bid their visitors farewell, Stuart Carver suddenly roused himself from a state of deep reflection. He jumped to his feet and placed a hand on Ebol's shoulder. "Son, would you be willing to carry a message to our sovereign?"

Ebol understood that Stuart's request was an opportunity for him to advance his mission on Earth. "Yes." He bowed respectfully to the guild president. "I would be honored to carry a message to your sovereign."

"It could be dangerous for you to get involved."

Ebol looked boldly into Stuart's eyes. "And it could be dangerous for the guild if I do not get involved. I'll go. I'm not afraid of danger."

Stuart smiled as one smiles admiringly at the face of valor. "Then go to Finngastoot and tell Sa Viddledass what you have seen here. Inform him that his regent has invited Zapin soldiers into Korasan. Tell him that the Jeefwood Forests are in peril."

A soldier appeared and shouted, "Visitors out."

While Ebol shook hands with Stuart, Lloyd ushered Lydia to the exit. "It's important Sa Viddledass hear of our situation. Do what you can to help Ebol with his travel arrangements."

"We are the people. We are the song. We are the truth that stands against wrong."

Lydia turned at the door and threw a parting glance at Aldersan. He caught her eye and smiled. Whether by intuition or by wishful thinking, she got the strange impression that he was thinking: We will dance again, I promise.

A breeze was blowing out of the northeast as Lydia and Ebol emerged from the warehouse. Lydia noted that the dark clouds she had seen earlier had grown in number, and it seemed likely to her that a storm was in the making. But before she could reflect on the weather, she and Ebol were surrounded by a throng of anxious women and children. Lydia happily informed them that the prisoners were in relatively good spirits.

Edbert appeared just as the crowd was dispersing, and joined Lydia, Glenda, Antoinette, Ella, and Ebol on a slow walk up Port Avenue. Although Antoinette did not actually treat Edbert with disdain, neither did she welcome him warmly.

Both Lydia and Ebol were in quiet, thoughtful moods. Ebol was still trying to absorb the idea that he was a figure in a legend, and Lydia was trying to figure out how to obtain Glenda's permission to go to Finngastoot with Ebol. She finally decided a direct approach was the best. So what if she altered the truth just a wee bit? "Mom. Stuart Carver asked Ebol to carry a message to Finngastoot, and Dad suggested that I go with Ebol."

Glenda stopped in her tracks and eyed Lydia dubiously. Even under the present circumstances, sending Lydia to

Finngastoot with a professional drifter did not sound like something Lloyd would suggest.

Lydia was not daunted by her mother's stare. "You told me to ask Dad if there was anything we could do. So I did. He wouldn't have suggested I go if it wasn't important that Stuart's message get through to the sovereign. Ebol is a foreigner. It might help if someone from Korasan travels with him."

Glenda pondered a moment, then said with a resigned shrug, "All right Lydia. If we must go to Finngastoot, we must."

"We?"

"Yes, we," replied Glenda. "Lydia, do you honestly expect me to let you travel so far alone."

Lydia pursed her lips and looked squarely into her mother's eyes. Instinct told her that this trip might have something to do the making of her own good future, and she sensed that she was not meant to travel to Finngastoot with her mother. "To begin with, Mom, I won't be alone. I'll be with Ebol, and he is an expert vagabond. He travels all the time. He just needs someone from Korasan to go with him. Besides, if you went, it would make the regent suspicious. You are the wife of a prisoner. Why would you be going to Finngastoot? He wouldn't think twice about me."

Glenda was forced to admit that there was some logic to Lydia's argument. Also, she was not all that keen on being so far from her imprisoned husband. Finally, reluctantly, with a very doubtful shake of her head, she relented. "All right Lydia, you may go. But how do you propose to get there? Even on a fast horse, it's a two- or three-day ride from Valerton to Finngastoot. If you walked, it might take a week."

Lydia shrugged. She had not yet thought so far ahead.

Edbert had been eavesdropping on Lydia and Glenda, and he now perceived an opportunity to redeem himself in Antoinette's eyes. "Excuse me for butting in," he said politely to Glenda. "But it's possible to sail from here to Finngastoot in ten or twelve hours. If my services might be accepted, I could take Lydia and Ebol in one of my father's numerous skiffs."

"Great!" Lydia exclaimed. "How soon can we leave?"

Edbert could see out of a corner of his eye that Antoinette and Ella Bell seemed favorably impressed by his offer. Assuming a new aura of professionalism, he wet a fingertip, held it in the air, and announced, "At the moment there is a good wind blowing in the right direction. If we were to leave soon, we could cover lots of water today, camp overnight, and arrive on the Finngastoot peninsula by late tomorrow morning."

"What if there's a storm?" asked Glenda.

Edbert glanced quickly at the sky before decreeing, "Those clouds will blow over."

"How soon is soon?" Lydia blurted. She was anxious to confirm a time of departure.

Edbert pondered a moment. His father had instructed him not to get involved in the protest, but he had said nothing about sailing to Finngastoot. "Give me a couple of hours to prepare one of the skiffs. Meet me by the north jetty at high noon."

Lydia turned to her mother, who nodded her consent, then turned excitedly to Ebol. "Does that suit you?"

"Better than these clothes," Ebol joked, yet he did so without any humor in his heart. He was terrified at the concept of boats at sea. The last nautical journey he had taken had not gone as expected.

Antoinette suddenly saw Edbert in a new light. She sidled over to him and cooed, "You know, sometimes you are too brave and considerate for words."

Edbert grinned proudly. "Thank you for noticing."

Edbert left to make arrangements for the boat. Ebol explained that he had some urgent business that needed attention before they sailed. The others proceeded toward the Bells' house to help Lydia pack for the trip.

After they had gone, Ebol wandered along the docks until he found the northernmost jetty. Next to it was a small pier, on the end of which was a large pile of cotton fishing nets. It did not take him long to arrange the nets into the general shape of a cloud bed and settle down to the pressing enterprise of snoozing.

Meanwhile, some fifteen leagues to the south and west of Valerton, the regent was standing in the field behind the Swains' cottage. His racing carriage had made the trip in a mere two and a half hours. As he stood admiring the spectacle of the Jeefwood Forest, he rubbed his chubby hands together and envisioned the profits that would soon be his. Judging from the look of ecstasy on the regent's face, his guards thought he was having a religious experience and they respectfully withdrew to the far side of the field. It was because of this withdrawal that not a single soldier saw Weezie until after she had grabbed the seat of the retreating regent's velvet pants. In Weezie's little waterfowl mind she was thinking, How dare you stand in the open when I'm patrolling my territory.

⇛18

In heaven there are no calendars to mark the passing of days, or weeks, or months, or years; there is only a glass bell that dings once each century. To a celestial being, time is like a river flowing endlessly to the sea. They have more of the stuff than they should ever need or want. To a human being, almost the opposite is true. For those of us bound to Earth, time is like a puddle, or a pond, or a lake if we are lucky. Accordingly, we treat time as a finite commodity, dividing and measuring its passing like so many hunchbacked accountants tallying flecks of precious gold. We are afraid it will slip by unnoticed and leave us dangling somewhere between the past and the present.

As the angel Natalie peered down over Korasan, the calendars on the walls indicated that it was two days before first-summer, and the sundials were casting shade lines just beyond the noon marker. Natalie felt somewhat relieved as she took stock of the principals involved in the Lydia Swain case. Some, of course, were in better shape than others, but she was satisfied that events were tending in the right direction.

Checking the warehouse, Natalie noted that the men were resting on full stomachs, relaxing to the sonorous strains of the bittersweet ballad that Lloyd Swain was whistling. Thanks to her vibratory ministrations, their wounds were mending rapidly. She was actually rather proud of the job she had done on Aldersan Hale's back. Except for a few tender welts, it was almost completely healed. At this moment, he was sitting in a darkened corner, staring forlornly at the window. Now that he had seen Lydia again, he suffered from an intense yearning to return to his studio and resume work on the unfinished sculpture. His hands literally itched to grab his tools and release her features from the jeefwood.

It struck Natalie that Aldersan was made more handsome by his yearning. Although she was an innocent angel, free of mortal desires, it was clear to her why Lydia had become infatuated with the fellow. Call it a crush, or call it divine attraction; Natalie would be watching over Aldersan long after the events of this story have been done and told.

Natalie turned her gaze up the hill toward the center of town, where Lydia Swain could be found in the Bells' dining room. Lydia was eating a hot meal before departing on her journey. At her feet sat Walter. He was not happy with village life; it seemed dogs were not allowed to go anywhere. At Lydia's side was Antoinette. Although she wished only for the safe success of Lydia's trip, Antoinette was a tad envious of her flaxen-haired cousin. As she saw it, Lydia was about to assume an important role in the theater of life, and if she triumphed in that role, she would return to Valerton a heroine. Antoinette could not imagine a better fate. Oh, glory of glories, she mused, what I would give to be adored and feted by all society! Along these lines she began to daydream. By the time Lydia ended her meal, Antoinette was already anticipating what she would wear to the public tribute.

Meanwhile, Edbert Sands (having fibbed wildly about his intentions) had managed to borrow one of his father's older, less-rentable sailing-skiffs. It was a sleek craft, built for speed rather than stability. Earlier Edbert had replaced the line that fastened the staysail to the top of the mast, and he was now hurriedly caulking several questionable seams he had discovered along the planks of the aged craft.

Natalie began to giggle when she found Ebol on the pier, sleeping atop the pile of fishing nets. Between heaven and Earth, some things never change. There he was, curled up in a ball, doing what he did best. Natalie's giggle exploded into a guffaw. A playful part of her wished that angels wore clothes in heaven, and that Ebol would return wearing the snazzy outfit that Edbert had lent him.

For the record, the angel Ebol was dreaming that he was ensconced in a sovereign-sized bed, surrounded by a hundred goose-down pillows.

Some time later, out of a corner of her eye Natalie spotted the regent's coach speeding east along the lane into Valerton. What she saw in the coach tickled her even more than Ebol's ludicrous attire. Victor Bimm was perched upon two seat cushions, and he winced painfully at every bump in the lane. Not only was the man's bottom-side aching, but his pride was hurt as well. Although he had commanded his soldiers to slaughter the mad goose that attacked him, the wily creature had vanished into the forest and managed to avoid detection.

Ebol was drawn from the comfort of his sweet dreams by the sound of his name flitting past him on the wind. It was Lydia. She had seen him sleeping on the nets. When he sat up, he saw her waving for him to hurry. Antoinette was standing on the end of the jetty, reaching to accept a piece of rope from Edbert. He was standing in the rear of a small skiff.

The wind buffeted Ebol sideways as he walked toward the end of the jetty, but it did not divert his gaze from the dubious-looking craft that Edbert had appropriated for their journey. At a glance, it was not the sort of boat that inspired confidence in a potential voyager. Indeed, the sight of the aging wooden conveyance sent cold shivers running through Ebol's bones. Lydia greeted Ebol cheerfully, "Good to see you. Did you attend to your urgent business?"

"All done." Ebol did not take his gaze from the craft. "Hey, Edbert. Are there any sharks in the Brillian Sea?"

Edbert shook his head. "Sharks? Never heard of them. What are they, some kind of fish?"

"More or less," Ebol muttered worriedly.

Edbert gestured proudly at the skiff. "What do you think? She may not be pretty, but she's fast."

Ebol eyed the craft sadly, then moaned and turned his gaze out to sea. A part of him was tempted to say "Bernard" three times and retreat immediately into the sanctuary of heaven. Yet he did not so much as mutter the letter B. If there was anything he feared more than a nautical journey in a derelict dinghy it was the prospect of standing before a disappointed seraph named Charlotte. He knew she would not look lightly upon a failed mission. As he gazed over the choppy, wind-blown water, he could hear Charlotte's words as clearly as if she were standing beside him: *Many subtle forces will hang in the balance when you enter the mortal world. Maintaining that balance will be your responsibility.*

The dinghy—which Edbert optimistically called a skiff—was roughly twelve feet long and four feet wide. In its center stood a ten-foot mast with a small, stable staysail at the top. Below this hung a larger mainsail attached to a movable boom. A line running through a pulley on the boom was used to draw the sail in and out. For seating, there were narrow planks laid across the breadth of the craft. Two oarlocks were mounted on either side, and oars hung on hooks attached to the ribs. In the stern was a crooked stick for steering the craft.

Ebol took another long look at the dinghy, then heaved a rather fatalistic sigh. He was willing to admit that in its day the craft may have been a source of pride for someone. Yet this admission provided him with no consolation whatsoever: The old wooden contraption simply did not invite confidence. It had originally been painted the same bright yellow as the shirt Ebol was wearing, but—unlike the shirt, which was still bright—the boat was covered with scum and algae growth, and was now very close to the color of a sun-baked bullfrog.

After exchanging a farewell hug with Antoinette, Lydia climbed into the bow of the craft and stuffed her traveling gear under the prow. When she did, she found a bucket, which she lifted and held out for Edbert's inspection. "What's this for?"

"Oh, that," Edbert remarked casually. "It's there for washing fish, or bailing out water if it rains."

Lydia replaced the bucket. Then, unable to suppress herself, she asked, "Edbert, are you sure this boat is seaworthy?"

Edbert was standing in the stern, shifting his weight from foot to foot in an effort to keep the boat balanced. He frowned at Lydia. "Do I look like the kind of fellow who would set out to Finngastoot in a skiff that was not seaworthy?"

"Sorry," Lydia said meekly. "It's just that I've never been in a boat before. And . . . well, the sea looks rather rough today."

Edbert addressed Lydia in the most reassuring tone he could muster. "It's true that these conditions might be dangerous in the hands of an amateur. But I've been plying these waters since I was a child. There is no need to concern yourself while Edbert Sands is at the helm."

Ebol was not impressed by Edbert's swank confidence. In fact, if Ebol could have had his druthers, he would have returned to the soft pile of fishing nets. But, of course, he could not shirk his higher duty. After all, as he reminded himself, he was a legendary figure in the history of the Farroupe lineage, and it was now incumbent upon him to deliver an important message to a member of that noble bloodline. Like it or not, the mission was his. He shook hands with Antoinette, then climbed into the boat and sat on a narrow thwart beside the mast. He had to lean forward to avoid contact with the boom.

Once his passengers were settled, Edbert bowed to Antoinette and said in a rather deep, melodramatic voice, "Keep well, my dear. We shall meet again."

"Bye, Edbert."

"Now, Antoinette, if you will, untie that line and toss it to me."

"Say please."

"Okay, please," Edbert said with strained patience.

Antoinette did as she was asked, yet when she tossed the docking line, it accidentally veered wide of the skiff and landed in the sea. Before bending to fetch the errant line, Edbert tied the tiller so that it would not move. But as he leaned to grab the line from the water, a gust of wind caught the mainsail. Then four things happened in rapid sequence. The boom swung around and hit Edbert squarely in the back. Edbert was propelled headfirst into the sea. The sail filled out. The skiff shot forward.

"Holy gamoly!" cried Ebol.

By the time Edbert resurfaced and wiped the saltwater from his eyes, the skiff had traveled thirty yards south and east of the jetty. Although he started to swim, he already knew it was highly unlikely that he would catch up with the runaway craft. The wind in the staysail alone was enough to carry the skiff. Even so, he continued to swim for another hundred yards. He was not all that eager to return to shore and hear Antoinette's opinion of the incident.

"Oh, lord!" Lydia screamed. "What do we do?"

Ebol did not hear Lydia. His head was jammed between his knees and he was rueing the moment he had first set eyes on the angel Natalie. In his mind it was because of her that he was now entagled in this mortal imbroglio. He could just imagine her: safely ensconced on a tranquil cloud, giggling at his fate.

The wind quickly filled out the sail. A knot on the line attached to the boom caught in the pulley and held the sail taut. The dinghy rolled in the water, and then—as swiftly as the wind that whipped over the choppy sea—the dirty yellow craft zipped along in a southeasterly direction.

In the five minutes it took for Lydia to recover her composure, crawl to the rear of the skiff, and grab the tiller, Valerton had become a blurred shape in the rapidly receding distance. Lydia experimented with the tiller, and after a few frantic moments she began to get a feel for how it influenced the skiff's motion. To her right lay the coast, and the first thing she did was try to turn in that direction. Unfortunately, though, the offshore wind was strong against her, and she barely managed to keep the craft parallel with the land. Having never been in a boat before, she did not know how to tack into the wind. Also, she had yet to figure out that letting out the mainsail would slow their wild passage.

Eventually Ebol lifted his head and peeked around. When he spotted brave Lydia at the helm of the runaway craft, he felt suddenly ashamed of his own cowardice. Here he was, being saved by the true-feeling supplicant who had appealed to him for help. It was behavior beneath the dignity of a proper angel. "Lydia, how might I assist you?"

"I don't know what you can do," Lydia cried. "I'm not sure what to do myself."

Ebol, anxious to do something, stood up—yet when he did, he stumbled and fell upon the mainsheet. The line tightened, the boom swung in, the skiff turned abruptly, stalled for an instant, then resumed its rapid pace.

The incident presented Lydia with some insight into how things worked on the boat. "Ebol. See if you can pull that line in far enough for me to grab hold of that wooden pole."

Ebol tugged on the line, and soon Lydia was able to grab the rudder stick. Because she was a country girl, she was strong enough to pull it across the stern. As she did, she saw that the skiff assumed a more level keel on the water. It also began to slow down a little.

Lydia tried again to navigate west toward the shore, but the wind was still much too strong, and she made no progress in that direction.

After Ebol disentangled himself from the line, he crawled back to assist Lydia. "Here," he said. "I'll hold this while you steer."

"You mean try to steer," Lydia corrected. "This thing isn't·

going where I want it to. All I'm managing to do is keep us in sight of land."

"Land is good."

"Finngastoot is that way." Lydia pointed with her nose. "At least we are heading in the right direction."

ᚦ19

Lydia and Ebol said little to each other during the next hour, as the runaway skiff continued its hurried passage over the whitecapped water. With every moment that passed free of mishap, their fear of the situation dwindled a degree, until eventually they actually started to feel optimistic about their chances for survival. Neither had a clue as to when or where their voyage might end, but at least now they were encouraged to hope for the best.

Again Ebol thought about his role in the whole episode, and again he felt ashamed of his own cowardly attitude. He knew it was foolish for him to worry about his own fate, especially considering that his status as a celestial being had already been established.

I've died and been given eternal life, he silently berated himself. What have I got to lose? Lydia is the one who matters here. She is the one who harbors the potential to act with the true feeling. She is the one whose fate has not yet been determined. It is my duty to remain calm and to help answer her prayer. There is nothing in this world that can harm my soul . . . not even this wild, stormy sea.

By the end of their second hour at sea, practical-minded Lydia had grown so confident with her ability to control the skiff that she began to experiment with the tiller and the mainsail. First she steered the craft in a wide, sweeping arc that carried them slightly closer to shore. Then she aimed the bow due west toward land and maneuvered the craft on a side-to-side, zigzag course. From this she gained enough knowledge to develop her own theory about tacking against the wind. Although she did not know the proper terms for her actions, she understood that she should pull the sail in tight and steer as close to the wind as possible, then luff and heel, then steer again into the wind.

And yet Lydia chose not to employ her new theories at this time. Instead, she aimed the skiff due south and continued sailing parallel with the land. As long as they were heading in the general direction of Finngastoot, she saw no need to alter their course.

Thus—their clothes and faces wet with spray and their hair tangled by the wind—the duo sailed on.

As the second hour gave way to a third, and then a fourth, a silent, respectful sort of awe settled over the two unlikely sailors. They kept company with their own inner reflections and held their gazes straight ahead. It was almost as if they were afraid that talking would disturb their felicitous momentum.

Later, after almost five hours at sea, as the first signs of early evening tinted the stormy sky, Lydia finally decided it was time to employ her theory and guide the skiff to shore.

By this juncture both she and Ebol were beginning to believe that luck was with them. It almost seemed as if they had everything under control.

"Ebol." Lydia's voice broke the long silence. "I'm going to try to take us in. Slowly, as I turn us toward the west, you pull that stick to your left. If you can, keep a little wind in the sail. But don't let it fill out completely."

"Aye, aye, captain." Ebol's voice was almost cheerful. He too had gotten a feel for how the skiff operated.

It is strange how life so often acts like a dream: At the moment you think you know what is coming next, it changes most dramatically. Before Lydia could perform the first zig in her intended zigzag, a low-pitched rumble of thunder reverberated in the eastern sky. The thunder was punctuated by the crackling sound of nearby lightning. There was a second of haunting silence, and then the whispering wind began to scream.

Ebol gripped the boom with all his might. There was another rumble of thunder, after which huge raindrops began to splatter the sea. The storm that been brewing all day had finally arrived.

Almost instantly the sea gave birth to a riot of unruly waves and the boat began rocking from side to side. Lydia soon discovered that her efforts with the tiller no longer had any effect on the skiff's activities. Within a matter of seconds, the hapless vessel began to birl, bob up and down, and ride wildly out of control.

As the world around her became a blur of wind, waves, and rain, Lydia's mind raced to the warehouse where her father and Aldersan Hale were imprisoned. The thought that she might never see them again was too excruciating to bear. She moaned, then turned her eyes toward heaven. *Please, if you are listening now, look down and still this storm. We are on a mission to save the Jeefwood Forest, and to do so we must survive. Please, look down and calm this storm.*

Ebol could hear fragments of Lydia's prayer, but before he could regret that he was not above to hear her words, a powerful gust of wind caught the sail and yanked the boom from his aching hands. Then—much to his and Lydia's horror—the boom broke, the mainsheet tore free, and the mast snapped cleanly in half.

And as if this latest twist of fate was not enough to completely humble the luckless sailors, two waves simultaneously hit the skiff. One pummeled the bow as the other slapped against the starboard side. The passengers were thrown forward into the body of the skiff, then promptly doused with gallon upon gallon of green water. Lydia's reaction was immediate. She crawled forward to the prow, grabbed the bucket that was lodged there, and began bailing as fast as she could bail.

At least the bucket was in good repair. After Lydia bailed for ten minutes, Ebol assumed the task. The whole time the skiff continued rocking from side to side, dipping up, dipping down, and spinning end around end. After many frantic minutes most of the seawater had been scooped from the hull and tossed back where it belonged. Then, partly to balance the craft and partly to avoid being tossed around, Ebol and Lydia lay crossways in the boat and braced their feet against the sides. They were doing the only thing that was left to do: hold on and hope they would survive the harrowing circumstances that gripped them.

It seemed to Lydia that it would take a miracle to save them. The minutes marched by like angry monsters and the storm showed no signs of abating. With a sharp stab of emotion she began to long for the safety and serenity of the Jeefwood Forest. She knew that only a few days before, she had been lamenting the boring routine of her lonely life, but now—and the irony of her changed attitude was not lost on her—no place in the world seemed as appealing as good old home. Now she wanted nothing more than to tend her precious jeeflets, roam the woods with Walter, and be content in the company of her parents.

They held on for one rainy hour, then another, and still they were alive. Soon night arrived and blanketed the storm-dimmed sky with utter darkness. A short while later Lydia heard something so out of place and unexpected, she could hardly believe her ears. In spite of the wild, rocking motion of the boat—not to mention the rain, or the fact that they were adrift at night on a stormy sea—Lydia's shipmate, the vagabond Ebol, had begun to snore. How, she wondered, did he find the peace of mind necessary to fall asleep in a tempest? Was he so relaxed about their prospects?

Of course, Lydia had no certain knowledge of eternal life, and so the concept of dying at sea bore the weight of a final judgment. She could hardly bear to imagine what might happen in the next moment, or the moment after that. Unlike Ebol, she could not presume that all would be well in the end.

Eventually the rain began to slack off. Afterward the wind quit screaming and the waves began to shrink. As the conditions grew more calm, so did the exhausted Lydia. Soon her show-me-a-challenge-and-I'll-meet-it human heart started pumping the tonic of blind faith through her veins. *Thump*, it said; *you are going to make it. Thump.* Meanwhile, at her side, she could hear the rise and fall of her shipmate's somnolent breathing.

After a lulling series of therapeutic thumps, Lydia yawned. Granted, it was physical and mental exhaustion that dragged her toward dreamland—not peace of mind. Nevertheless, dreamland was where she was headed.

While Lydia drifted (at sea and to sleep), Ella and Willard Bell were in their second-floor guest room tending to Ella's sister, Glenda Swain. Glenda knew only that her daughter was lost at sea in a storm. The rest of her thoughts were confused by a crippling fear of what she did not know. Throughout the day and into the evening she had been assailed by guilt for having given Lydia permission to make the journey in the first place, and now she had slipped into a state of consciousness that lay somewhere between sleep and cataleptic shock.

On the floor above, Antoinette sat at her bedroom window, peering into the abysmal night. Although she was worried about Lydia and Ebol, her thoughts were currently on Edbert Sands. She had recently decided that she could not forgive herself for the way she had behaved toward him earlier in the day. He had only been trying to help, and yet she had treated him like a smelly fish. First, when he swam back to the jetty, she had called him an idiot, and then, after he obtained a second boat and went after the runaway skiff, only to be driven back to shore by the storm, she informed him that he would never again enjoy the pleasure of her company. Her heart sank as she recalled the fallen expression on his face. Poor thing. He had looked sadder than a wet dog with no tail and no place to call home.

As Antoinette lamented her heartlessness, the object of her shame sat shivering in a shed at the north end of Valerton. While he listened to the agitated sea, he questioned whether it would be in his best interest to continue living or not. As he saw it, his actions had put two lives at risk—if indeed they were still alive. And now the girl he loved had sworn to avoid him forever. Also, it seemed quite likely that his father would soon disown him, or worse.

Although Edbert did not know it, the angel Natalie was keeping a keen eye on the shed. Thus there was never any real chance that he would give up on life.

Lydia had no idea of how long she had slept. She could not remember falling asleep. She could not remember having any dreams. The first thing she saw when she opened her eyes was a scarlet streak of dawn peeking out under a shelf of slate-gray clouds. The storm had passed. The sea was calm.

Lydia heard the gentle splash of an oar entering the water. When she lifted her head, she saw Ebol's back. He was sitting on a makeshift plank seat, bent forward. He drove each oar into the water. Lydia pulled herself into a sitting position. In the near distance she saw a finger of land jutting into the sea. "Ebol. Good morning."

"Hi, sleepyhead."

"Oh my gosh, look," exclaimed Lydia. "There's a town at the end of that peninsula."

"I know."

"Do you think it's Finngastoot?"

"I'm not turning around if it isn't," Ebol said with a robust laugh. He was rather tickled with his own performance.

⇥20

Call it luck, say it was the result of fortitude, attribute the outcome to fate, credit providence, or simply accept the fact: Early in the morning on the day before first-summer in Korasan, Lydia Swain and the vagabond Ebol climbed from their borrowed (now battered) dinghy onto a pebble-strewn beach near the town of Finngastoot. As the two adventurers dragged their vessel toward high ground, three local fishermen happened to look up from the nets they were mending and observe the arriving party. They were intrigued by the broken skiff, as well as fascinated by Ebol's attire.

Ebol, flush with the pride of his recent accomplishment, smiled broadly at the fishermen. "Hello, my fellow mariners. That sure was one heck of a storm last night."

There was an astonished pause. The fishermen glanced

at the storm-wracked dinghy, shook their heads with dis-belief, then turned their wide-eyed gazes back to Lydia and Ebol. Finally, one of the men inquired, "Where are you hailing from?"

"I'm from Valerton," answered Lydia. "And he's from Yegopt. We've come to speak with Sa Viddledass. Would you be so kind as to direct us to his residence?"

The eldest of the fishermen rubbed his weathered face before pointing. "Straight up yonder avenue, young lady. The sovereign lives in the sand-colored house with the high fence and the guards at the gate. You would have to be blind to miss it."

"Thank you, sir," Lydia said politely. She may have looked like a shipwrecked mess, but she had not forgotten her manners.

"You are welcome," said the old man. "But today marks the beginning of the first-summer holiday, and I do believe the sovereign will not be receiving visitors until next week."

"Oh," remarked the newly emboldened Ebol. "We shall just have to see about that."

Before entering the town, Lydia retrieved her travel bag from beneath the prow. In it was a comb, a hand mirror, and an ornamental broach her mother had given her to wear. After making herself somewhat presentable (there was nothing she could do about her wet dress), she handed the comb and mirror to Ebol. He winced when he saw his reflection. During the excitement of the voyage he had forgotten what he was wearing.

Finngastoot was the oldest known settlement in all of

Korasan. It had been the home of the country's first sovereign, and was now the largest village in all the land. Yet as Lydia and Ebol proceeded up its main avenue, they were not particularly impressed by what they saw. There were more shops, more houses, more carriages, and more people in Finngastoot than in Valerton, but otherwise the place seemed no more exciting.

Lydia and Ebol were impressed by the eight soldiers guarding the gate to the sovereign's residence. Each one of them was tall and broad shouldered. All of them were attired in baggy red-and-gold uniforms. All of them had swords at their sides.

The guards scrutinized the messengers from Valerton with the same suspicious gazes they aimed at all uninvited visitors. When Lydia asked if she and Ebol might speak with the sovereign, the reply she received was so succinct it might have been interpreted as rude: "No."

Looking through the fence and across the lawn, Lydia could see a bearded, white-haired man sitting on a bench on a veranda outside the royal residence. He wore a purple robe. On his head was a maroon-and-gold cap. It did not take much imagination for Lydia to suppose that she was looking at Sa Viddledass. "But sir," Lydia addressed the soldier nearest her, "we came from Valerton in the storm. My friend carries an important message to the sovereign. It's from the president of the Artisan Guild."

"No visitors are welcome until one week after first-summer."

"You don't understand," Lydia pleaded. "We are not visitors; we are messengers."

An unsympathetic grunt was the reply Lydia received.

"Please," Lydia persisted. "I'm sure when Sa Viddledass hears what we have to say, he will be glad you let us in."

The soldier shrugged with stoic indifference.

Ebol did not like the way the soldiers were treating Lydia. He stepped forward and confronted the guards with a look of stern reproach. "Tell your sovereign that an ambassador from Yegopt has come to pay him a call."

The forward-most soldier replied to Ebol with a swift lifting of a sword, which he pointed menacingly. "Never heard of the place. Now scat, or you will be arrested."

"Scat yourself," retorted Ebol. "We are on a mission and we will not be dismissed by some low-ranking gate guard."

Lydia was alarmed by Ebol's behavior. She grabbed the back of his jacket and pulled him away from the entrance. "You must be careful here, Ebol. If we get arrested, it will ruin our chances for you to deliver Stuart Carver's message. And if you don't . . ." She slumped and frowned worriedly. "Poor Dad and Aldersan and everyone else in Valerton."

"Don't fret, Lydia," Ebol said with aplomb. He was not absolutely sure if this was the right time, but he was certain it was the right place. "I'll deliver the message."

"How? It doesn't look like they're going to let us in."

Ebol could feel both the heaviness of Lydia's disappointment and the burden of Charlotte's mandate: *Help Lydia Swain resolve the conflict that threatens her world.* "We will not be detained much longer."

"We won't?"

"Nope," Ebol replied emphatically. "Now, follow me."

"What are you going to do?" Lydia asked fearfully, but

Ebol did not reply. The truth was that he had not yet decided what to do; he only knew that he intended to act.

Lydia was completely mystified by her companion. In the brief time they had known each other, she had come to think of Ebol as a rational individual with mellow manner, but it now appeared he was about to do something foolish. "Wait," she called. "I want to know what you are going to do."

"Just watch," Ebol said over his shoulder as he strode toward the gate. Even he was astonished by his bold behavior. Something inside him that he could not name had risen up and was impelling him toward the soldiers.

The soldiers glared at him as if he were in immediate danger. But then, before they could decide who among them would grab the disrespectful foreigner, Ebol cupped his hands to his mouth and hollered across the lawn, "Yo, Sa Viddeldass! I've come from Yegopt to spea—" The rest of Ebol's message was interrupted by a strong arm that grabbed him around the neck. Before he was thrown to the ground and muffled with a kerchief, he managed to bite the arm and cry, "Yegopt!"

When Lydia tried to rush to Ebol's side, she also met with a strong arm. While it held her, she watched one of the guards roll Ebol onto his stomach and lash his wrists with rawhide.

Although Sa Viddledass's sensory receptors were not as sharply tuned as they had once been, he was aware of the scuffle taking place at his gate, and he thought he had heard the word "Yegopt." Having been sovereign since he was nineteen, he was used to making quick decisions. He rang a bell to signal a house guard, then sent the man to investigate. "If those youngsters claim to hail from Yegopt, bring them to me. Otherwise have them taken away."

A moment later, Lydia and Ebol were ushered across the lawn by a pair of unhappy guards. They stopped five yards from where Korasan's sovereign sat on a cushioned bench. The old ruler inspected the visitors with a questioning gaze, then ordered the guards to untie Ebol's hands and remove themselves. Not only had his years as sovereign taught him to make quick decisions, they had also given him the ability to judge character at a glance. It was clear to him that Lydia and Ebol had honest intentions. He rested a royal-blue eye on Ebol and asked, "Did I hear you say you were from Yegopt?"

"Yes, sir. I mean, yes, Mr. Sovereign."

Sa Viddledass smiled benignly and turned to Lydia. "You have the look of a Korasanian. Is that so?"

"Yes, my sovereign." Lydia trembled shyly. "I am from the countryside, near Valerton."

"Please, come forward and sit beside me."

Ebol was awestruck as he sat down on the sovereign's left. Over two hundred years had passed since he had last seen such intense cobalt-blue eyes. Surely here was proof that Stuart Carver's story about the sovereign's ancestor was true. As much as he could remember the pregnant woman's eyes, he now saw them peering at him again.

"Yegopt." Sa Viddledass let the word dangle in the air for a ponderous moment. "I first heard of Yegopt when I was a child half your age. It is a land I have always wanted to visit. If you would, tell me about that fair country."

"Well, sir . . . Mr. Sovereign. It has been quite a while since I was there. What exactly would you like to know?"

"Anything you care to tell me."

"Anything?"

The sovereign paused to consider before replying, "I suppose I should like to know how your society is structured."

"Structured? Hmmm." Ebol frowned and struggled to collect his thoughts on the subject. But he was promptly distracted by Lydia. She had leaned forward and was glaring at him. Her eyes were open wide and she was silently mouthing words. Lydia was making it abundantly clear that he should quit dallying and deliver Stuart Carver's message.

Sa Viddledass noticed the silent dialogue going on around him. He glanced at Lydia, then asked Ebol, "What does she say?"

Ebol winced with embarrassment at having gotten sidetracked. "I have an important message to you from a man named Stuart Carver. He is the president of the Artisan Guild in Valerton."

"I know who Stuart is," noted the sovereign. "What does he have to say?"

As Ebol imparted his message and attempted to explain the situation in Valerton, Korasan's thoughtful ruler listened with a patient air. In those instances when Ebol's knowledge of the facts faltered, Lydia supplied the missing information.

After Ebol's tale was told (including a very colorful account of their night voyage across the stormy Brillian Sea), Sa Viddledass furrowed his brow and sighed.

When the sovereign sighed, Lydia flashed on the fortune-teller's prophecy: *I see a sleeping stranger. I see a stormy sea. I see a sovereign sighing. Behold! There is a kiss beneath a jeefwood tree.* She suddenly grew giddy with wonder. In the past week she had witnessed three of the four predictions. Would the fourth one soon come true?

Sa Viddledass reached for a bell at his side and rang it twice. With dazzling promptness one of his house guards appeared on the veranda and stood at attention. "My good sir," said the sovereign. "Find the captain of my elite troops and inform him that I want a hundred men ready to sail for Valerton in no less than two hours."

The guard saluted. "Will that be all?"

"Explain to the captain that we have a small problem with Valerton's regent. It seems he has allowed a brigade of foreign soldiers into Korasan. I have reason to suspect they are from Zapin. There might be a conflict."

The guard saluted again. "Anything else?"

Sa Viddledass nodded. "After speaking with the captain, find my chef and instruct him to prepare a platter for two hungry sailors. Have him deliver the food to my library."

"Yes, sovereign." The guard saluted a third time before departing.

As the guard hurried away, Sa Viddledass stood up from the bench and put a hand on Ebol's shoulder. "Let us repair to my library. I want to show you an old map of Yegopt that one of my ancestors drew over two hundred years ago."

Holy gamoly, thought Ebol. Surely the sovereign was speaking of the pregnant woman's husband. Now he was beginning to fathom the beautiful mystery of why he of all angels had been chosen to hear Lydia's prayers.

During the next ninety minutes, as the elite troops prepared for the trip to Valerton, Lydia, Ebol and Sa Viddledass waited in the royal library. For the most part, Lydia quietly nibbled at the platter of nuts, fruits, cheeses, pâtés, and breads. With half her mind she listened to Ebol and Sa Viddledass discuss a faraway land called Yegopt, and with the other half she ruminated about her imprisoned father, her jeeflets, and the possibilities of her own good future.

⤕21

Six long days had passed since Aldersan Hale was conked over the head and tossed into the regent's stone warehouse by the sea. Now he leaned against the east wall of his cell, staring at the small upper window. Tonight the patch of cloudless sky that he could see featured the bright full moon of first-summer.

Watching the window had become something of an obsession with Aldersan. For him it was a hole though which his mind could escape the harsh reality of his internment and wander freely in the spacious air of abstract reflection. For him the window was a place where his bitterness at being whipped no longer existed. When he was staring at the space, the only thing that really mattered was returning to his studio and resuming work on the sculpture of Lydia.

Once an artist, always an artist.

Likewise: Once a mother, always a mother. Over thirty hours had passed since Glenda was last certain of her daughter's safe whereabouts, and the strain of those hours had left her nearly crippled with anxiety. Her every moment was haunted by a keen sense of helplessness. She was quite willing to do whatever was needed to insure Lydia's well-being—she would give her own life if necessary—but all she could do now was wait. And wait. Her single consolation was the knowledge that Lloyd did not know of Lydia's missing status, and thus did not have to suffer more than he was already suffering as a prisoner.

Although Glenda's mind was too fraught with anguish to formulate an actual prayer, her indomitable human heart was able to shepherd her feelings into a wordless plea that was so intense, the angel Natalie could hear the thumping of Glenda's heart in heaven. The young celestial servant did her best to absorb Glenda's grief, transform it into faith, and beam the altered energy back to its source. Even for spunky little Natalie, this was no easy task.

Meanwhile, Lydia could only marvel as she stood on the upper deck of the sovereign's royal junker-ship and watched the moonlight shimmer on the undulating surface of the Brillian Sea. Below her she could hear forty oars slapping the silvery water, and off to her right she could see the shadowy shape of the troop carrier that was accompanying the sovereign's ship.

So much had happened recently that Lydia could hardly begin to put it all in perspective. In the past seven days she had met a sleeping stranger, participated in a demonstration against the regent, visited her jailed father, made eye contact with Aldersan Hale, survived a stormy night at sea, and become personal friends with the sovereign. And now . . . well, now it looked as if there might soon be a reasonable cause for celebration.

As Lydia stood on the upper deck, Korasan's benign ruler sat on the main deck discussing strategy with the captain of his elite troops. They were planning a predawn liberation of Valerton. Ebol had retired to the royal quarters, where he was currently asleep in the sovereign's own bed.

The events of the past several days soon caught up with Lydia, and she retired to one of the hammocks on deck. She was still sleeping some three hours later when the sovereign's twin junker-ships dropped anchor a mile south of Valerton. The captain sent a reconnaissance unit ashore, and while they were scouting the situation, the remaining troops prepared their gear and waited silently in the moonlight.

The advance unit returned within an hour. After a brief consultation with the captain and several top officers, the troops disembarked from their respective ships and traveled quickly ashore in long pontoons.

Having the sovereign's authority on their side, as well an advantage in numbers and the benefit of surprise, the royal troops managed to achieve their mission with exceptional dispatch. The soldiers from Zapin, finding themselves surrounded by a larger force, surrendered without a fight. They, after all, were hired men whose hearts were not in their jobs. The regent's personal troops also surrendered without a fight. Ultimately they were loyal to the sovereign. And so, without bloodshed and before the first day of first-summer had finished dawning, the good soldiers of Korasan had arrested the regent and released the seven unjustly jailed men from the warehouse.

Lloyd Swain paused long enough to thank the soldiers for freeing him from the smelly warehouse, then started running as fast as his tree-climbing legs could carry him. All he cared about at this moment was seeing his loving wife and daughter again.

"Who would be banging on our door at this hour?" Ella Bell sat up and asked her husband.

"I have no idea," Willard said shortly. "Whoever it is, he better not wake Glenda—not after what we went through getting her to fall asleep."

Ella climbed wearily out of bed and went to answer the door. She almost fainted when she saw Lloyd standing on the stoop. She paused for an instant, wondering how best to break the news about Lydia. While she was considering, Lloyd bolted past her and bounded up the stairs.

Glenda's conciousness was dancing fitfully around the edges of sleep when Lloyd entered the Bells' guest room and hurried to her side. She awoke instantly at the familiar, tender touch of his workman's hand. "Sweetheart," she gushed, then threw her arms around him and cried, "Lloyd,

I have the worst news in the world. Lydia has been lost at sea since yesterday."

"Lost?" Lloyd was stunned. He did not know that Lydia had gone with the Yegoptian lad to see the sovereign. "What? How?"

Somehow Glenda found the will to pull herself together and tell Lloyd what had happened. While he listened, he furrowed his brow and gazed questioningly into his wife's bleary eyes. Her voice sank sharply when she told how Lydia and Ebol had last been seen sailing into a storm on the runaway skiff.

"Glenda, did you say she went with the vagabond to deliver Stuart Carver's message to the sovereign?"

"Yes."

A broad smile abruptly appeared on Lloyd's face. "Then Lydia must have made it to Finngastoot. I was let out of the warehouse by members of the sovereign's elite troops."

When the logic of what Lloyd was implying penetrated the fog of Glenda's weariness, she made a noise that can only vaguely be approximated by words. It sounded something like a squeak, yet at the same time it was happy like a peep, shrill like a whistle, and drawn out like a squeal. Then Glenda began to shed a flood of pent-up tears.

Lloyd slid his arms around her waist and whispered, "There, there. Everything is going to be all right."

They did not have to wait long before Lloyd's words were confirmed as fact. Lydia had awoken at dawn that morning and was on the main deck, having tea and cake with the sovereign, when an officer arrived to report that the mission was a success. The news excited Lydia so much, she temporarily forgot her manners and spoke before Sa Viddledass had a chance to question the man. "Have the prisoners been let out of the warehouse?"

The soldier nodded yes.

In her joy Lydia rushed forward and hugged the sovereign. He winked at the waiting soldier. "Be a good man and take this young lady ashore immediately. I will come along in a while."

When Lydia reached the house on Lumber Lane, she did not bother to knock at the door. She simply burst into the front hallway and hollered, "Mom! Antoinette! It's me. I'm back."

Walter was the first to respond. He sprang from his basket in the kitchen, zoomed down the hall like a speeding greyhound, yapped ecstatically, and leapt into Lydia's arms.

"Hey, little fellow."

"*Arryap yap,*" said Walter. He was thinking: Where have you been? And when are we going home?

Lydia set Walter down just before Glenda ran and nearly knocked her over with a hug. "Oh, Lydia," Glenda sobbed, and wrapped her arms around her daughter. A second later Lloyd added his arms to the embrace. Then Antoinette, Ella, and Willard Bell appeared and huddled joyously around the Swains.

News of Sa Viddledass's presence in Valerton spread through the village faster than a whisper of good gossip. It

168

had been many years since the sovereign had ventured outside his home in Finngastoot, and the local citizenry considered it a high honor to receive the great personage. Due to the surprise nature of his visit, there was little time for the village leaders to prepare a proper welcome. Still, they did their best. By noon of that first day of first-summer in Korasan, a jeefwood podium had been erected in Valerton's central square and the entire ambulatory population of the village had gathered in jubilant anticipation.

While the crowd waited for Sa Viddledass, they were serenaded by Sophia Quirk, the whistling bird-girl. Only the people closest to the podium could actually see the dimunitive whistler in the cardinal-red dress, yet everyone in the square could hear her clearly. With arms flapping, she rocked to and fro on her heels and wowed the crowd with the strains of "There's a Mist on the Mountain."

Sa Viddledass was detained longer than expected by military matters and was late arriving in the square. A rumor that he was busy designing a unique punishment for the regent inspired much patience among the populace. Later, it was confirmed that the sovereign had revoked Victor Bimm's authority and ordered him to Finngastoot to work five years in the royal household as a dishwasher. It was also learned that Felix Drump's private soldiers would be ransomed back to the tycoon for twenty talens each. The money from this transaction would be used to establish a fund in memory of Bash Landy. The fund would be managed by the Artisan Guild and employed in the development of new jeefwood forests.

Finally, after two encores from the bird-girl (she had begun to turn slightly blue in the face), the well-loved sovereign of Korasan, Sa Viddledass, strolled into the square. Although he was surrounded by a phalanx of soldiers intended to protect him from the press of the crowd, the villagers behaved with such civilized decorum that the precaution proved unnecessary. The sovereign was accompanied by a small entourage consisting of Valerton's mayor, the Artisan Guild's president, and the vagabond from Yegopt.

There was no need for an introduction. Sa Viddledass simply approached the podium, and with a dignity and grace that cannot be taught, he bowed to the crowd. When he spoke, his elderly voice lacked volume, yet his words were enriched by a spirit of sincere love for his listeners. "Greetings. I wish you all a happy first-summer. It has been too long since I have visited here. I promise I shall not be so remiss in the future. Hopefully, when I return again, it will not be because you have been threatened by the deeds of someone who was meant to guard your welfare. By the way . . ." Sa Viddledass smiled knowingly. "That someone has been assigned elsewhere and will no longer represent me in Valerton. Henceforth that duty will be shared by Louise Spate and Stuart Carver. They have graciously agreed to act as my coregents."

Sa Viddledass bowed to Louise and Stuart and waited until the chorus of cheers had finished echoing over the square. Then he turned back to the crowd and continued, "Before I go, there are two courageous individuals who deserve to be honored. It is because of their actions that a great civil crime has been averted." The sovereign paused and searched the square, until he spotted Lydia standing with her parents. All eyes followed his gaze and settled upon the shy heroine.

Blood rushed to Lydia's cheeks when the sovereign said her name, and her knees wobbled when he thanked her for making the trip to Finngastoot. Unlike Antoinette, she did not relish the public eye. Lydia was proud of her achievement, but she preferred anonymity over acclaim. Fortunately for her nerves, the crowd soon turned its attention back to Sa Viddledass, who gestured for the vagabond from Yegopt to step forward.

Ebol was daydreaming when the sovereign signaled, and it was several seconds before he realized he had been beckoned. When he finally did step forward, Sa Viddledass rested a fraternal hand upon his shoulder and proclaimed: "This young fellow has been of great assistance to the Artisan Guild, as well as to the sovereignty of Korasan. Henceforth he shall be recognized as an honorary citizen of our country. Know him as my guest, and as my friend. His brave actions will long be remembered."

As the crowd began to cheer, Ebol—still half lost in a daydream—put his hand to his mouth to suppress a mighty yawn.

❧22

The next day, when the sovereign sailed for Finn-gastoot, he left a contingent of his elite troops in Valerton. Their purpose was to oversee the ransoming of Felix Drump's soldiers and to assist the new coregents as they made the transition to power. (The old regent was seen on the deck of the departing ship, wearing kitchen whites and an apron.)

During the next several days and nights the seaside village resounded with a plethora of cheers, laughs, shouts, and squeals. Community spirit was everywhere. At almost every turn citizens could be found winking, or smiling, and generally indulging in dollops of old-fashioned fun. Much mead was spilled and many backs were heartily patted.

Edbert Sands contributed heavily to the smile count. What he had initially thought was the dawn of a very bad year now seemed like the beginning of rather promising era. For one thing, his father had received so much praise for supplying the skiff that carried the messengers, he had revised his view of Edbert's character and decided he was quite proud of his son. Edbert was duly relieved by his father's change of heart, yet it seemed a paltry matter next to a certain auspicious event that occurred on the night of the sovereign's speech. It was an event punctuated by a moonlit kiss, bestowed by a suddenly adoring Antoinette

Bell. "Edbert," she whispered. "I've decided *not* to never speak to you again. In fact, I've been thinking of things I might say to you tomorrow, and the day after that."

Edbert broadened his already broad smile, reached into a hip pocket, and withdrew a bag of candied ginger.

"Oooh," Antoinette cooed appreciatively. "My favorite."

The next day, after breakfast with the Bells, the Swains joined the crowd that gathered on the docks to bid the departing sovereign farewell. After he was gone, they climbed into their wagon and started for home.

Late that afternoon, when the Swains arrived back at their cottage, they entered into an exceedingly busy period of work. Glenda did not even wait for the wagon to stop before she jumped from the buckboard and hurried to the barn, where her distressed cows were mooing to be milked. Lloyd also did not dally. The delayed harvest had been rescheduled for the fifth day of first-summer, which left him a mere three nights and two days to complete his preparations. (He was in such a panic over all there was to do, he had failed to whistle so much as a single note on the entire trip home.) Although Lydia was in much less of a rush than her parents, she did go to the garden shed to check her jeeflets before retiring to the comfort of her bedroom.

On the afternoon of the fourth day of first-summer, after nearly two days of hard work, Lydia excused herself from the endless chores and went to rest in her favorite forest grove. Walter, of course, went with her.

As Lydia reflected upon the recent events of her life, it was difficult for her to believe that only eight mornings had dawned since she and her parents had last left their cottage and traveled to Valerton. So much had happened so quickly; in retrospect it was all beginning to seem like an incredible dream. Of one thing, though, she was certain: She could no longer claim that her life had always been boring.

Intellectually, Lydia knew she should be happy. The guild had been saved, the forest would remain, her family's way of life was preserved, she had traveled, she had brought honor to the Swain name, and she was now on speaking terms with Sa Viddledass. And yet . . . she was not as joyous as she might have been.

Basically, there were three matters oppressing her soul. To begin with, there was a problem with her pet goose, Weezie. The old bird would not come home and she would not allow anyone to get near her. Since her return Lydia had seen Weezie on several occasions, but each time she tried to calm the goose with soft words, the crazy bird had honked angrily and fled into the forest.

A second matter weighing on Lydia's soul was the departure of Ebol. She had last seen him in the crowd that had gathered on the docks in Valerton to wave good-bye to Sa Viddledass. With her parents' permission she had invited Ebol to be a guest at their home. But he had declined and, with a hug, said it was time for him to return to his own world. She had discovered that she missed him more than could reasonably have been expected.

Those vagabonds and their wandering ways. She knew she would remember the sight of him waving farewell for many years to come.

The third matter oppressing Lydia concerned Aldersan Hale. Much to her keen disappointment, she had not seen him since two days before first-summer, when they had encountered each other in the warehouse. She had been convinced then that he was pleased to see her, but now she was beset with doubts she could not easily dismiss. They were based upon a plain and simple fact: In all the hours since Aldersan's release from the warehouse, he had made no attempt to see her again. He had not come to hear the sovereign speak, he had not shown his face in the square on the festive moonlit night of first-summer, and he had not been in the crowd that gathered the next day at the docks. Where had he been?

Ah, those artists and their independent ways—they are worse than vagabonds when it comes to the heart of things.

While Lydia sat ruminating on her rock, the first wave of guild workers arrived in the field behind the cottage. She could hear them unloading their wagons and setting up camp. Sadly, their presence on the property only served to heighten her emotional confusion. Again she reminded herself that she should be happy, yet she knew in her heart that she was not.

After a depressing little while Lydia's thoughts turned to the old fortune-teller. Soon she heard the sound of his voice whispering in her ear: *For all of us there awaits a good future or a less-good future. The purpose of life, of course, is to pursue the good future, and the instrument for doing so is belief.*

Recent experience had taught Lydia to respect the words of the old seer. So now, with genuine intent, she tried to determine exactly what she did believe, and what for her would constitute a good future.

Was is it really so simple? Was life really for the making and the very well made? If so, how was she to know the difference between the things she merely wanted to happen and the things she actually believed in? Were believing and wanting the same?

It did not take long before Lydia was utterly confused by a number of unanswerable questions. Feeling defeated, she sighed and turned her gaze toward the blue opening in the overhead canopy of green. *Please, I know you are up there. Help me find my good future. Please, answer my prayer.*

Aldersan Hale awoke with a start when the wagon came to a halt in the field. He had just slept for most of the day, but prior to this morning he had been awake for three days and three nights. All of that time had been spent in his studio. (He never did know what to make of the old clothes he found folded on his workbench.) He had finished the carving of Lydia at dawn, then raced to the square to join the harvest crew before they left for the Jeefwood Forest.

As Aldersan sat up and looked around, he felt a wave of excitement sweep through his body. For one thing, he had never seen a mature jeefwood tree—much less a forest of them—and for another, he knew he had now arrived at Lydia's home. He was slightly unnerved by the prospect of their meeting again. During his long hours of working with Lydia's image, he had developed a growing fondness for the girl. In time, he had realized he was smitten. The fondness, of course, resided in the chambers of his heart, and now that bold little muscle was pounding loudly.

Aldersan jumped from the wagon and began walking toward the great forest. He had no clue that the angel Natalie had watched him awaken, and subsequently he never suspected that the path he followed into the woods was not selected at random.

After seeing that Aldersan was aimed in the right direction, Natalie turned and raced toward the Karmatic Stairway. There was a favor she wished to ask of the great seraph Charlotte. Natalie had been following the events in Korasan much too closely to let the potentially romantic encounter between Lydia and Aldersan pass without a further heavenly nudge.

Lydia's ears perked when Walter began to growl. Then she heard footsteps crunching on the forest floor, and she turned. Her initial hope was that Ebol had changed his mind and decided to visit after all. Yet she quickly forgot about Ebol when she saw Aldersan approaching. "Hush," she whispered to Walter. In her cheeks she could feel the heat of a blush.

Aldersan was startled by the sight of Lydia sitting on the boulder, and it was not until after he had taken a deep breath that he found the composure to speak. "Excuse me. I hope I'm not interrupting you. I was just walking in the woods." After pausing for a reply, which did not come, he added, "And what marvelous woods they are."

Lydia had to untie her tongue before using it to speak. "I was just thinking. You're not interrupting anything."

Aldersan smiled kindly. "I'm Aldersan Hale."

"I know."

"I've seen you three times this year. This is the fourth."

Lydia did not know what to say, so she shrugged shyly and looked down. In the distance she could hear the guild workers laughing and calling to one another. Suddenly one of the voices began to sing an old dance tune called "Come Step with Me." Then a company of voices joined the singer.

Aldersan gave Walter a friendly glance and stepped forward. Walter quivered, then retreated toward the periphery of the clearing. "It was brave of you to take Stuart's message to the sovereign," Aldersan said sincerely.

"Oh, it was nothing," Lydia mumbled as she lifted eyes to meet his.

"Nothing? You saved the guild. . . ." Aldersan paused and looked around for effect. "You saved these magnificent jeefwoods."

Lydia shrugged modestly. "All I did was go with Ebol. He was responsible for delivering the message."

"Still, it was a brave thing you did," Aldersan insisted. He started to add something, then hesitated. A rather anxious expression appeared on his face, and he blurted, "Speaking of brave, I should be brave enough to tell you that I just finished sculpting a block of jeefwood in your likeness. And now that I see you again, well, I think I did a pretty good job of capturing you . . . if I do say so myself. Of course, it helped that I had such a beautiful model to work from."

Lydia could not hide her astonishment, or her pleasure.

The news that Aldersan thought she was beautiful had robbed her of the ability to speak. She felt captured indeed.

Aldersan was encouraged by Lydia's evident delight, and he began to relax. "I started on the carving soon after we met and danced at the spring festival," he said, shifting his weight and taking another step toward the boulder. "By the way, I remember the promise I made to you. I hope you didn't think I forgot."

Lydia felt a thunderbolt of joy shoot up her spine. Her soul was no longer oppressed. In the distance she could hear the workers singing "Come Step with Me."

Aldersan timidly extended an open hand. "Would you care to dance with me now?"

"Yes, I would," Lydia answered with flashing eyes. As she slid off the boulder, she reminded herself: One step sideways, one step back, one step sideways, one step forward.

Ebol was dreaming that he was riding upon a cushioned litter at the head of a hero's parade when he was abruptly awoken by the impact of a pointed foot striking his buttocks. When he opened his eyes, there was a gleam in them that left little doubt about his opinion of the incident. "Holy gamoly, Natalie. What now?"

"I thought you might want to see what is happening below."

"What?" Ebol said flatly. He showed no sign that he was prepared to look anywhere.

"Your friend Lydia and the artist Aldersan are alone in the forest together."

Ebol's face revealed a small sign of interest.

179

"Maybe they need a little help getting to know each other."

Ebol turned down the corners of his mouth in a frown. "Maybe they do. Maybe they don't. What do you have behind your back?"

Natalie grinned mischievously and exposed the golden bow and arrow she was holding. "It took some fast talking on my part, Ebol, but I got permission for you to return to Korasan for one earthly minute. This arrow will ensure that there is a kiss beneath a jeefwood tree. Charlotte said to tell you be careful when you aim."

Ebol grimaced and rolled over on his stomach. And then, since he just happened to be in this position, he decided to allow himself a quick peek into the Jeefwood Forest. He was rewarded with a view of Lydia and Aldersan dancing slowly together.

"Come on, Ebol," Natalie persisted. "It's all set up. Charlotte said you just have to whisper the word 'Korasan' and you'll be there. Then all you have to do is hit Lydia or Aldersan with the arrow."

Ebol sat up and looked at Natalie, yet did not speak.

"If you go, I promise I'll let you sleep a hundred years."

Ebol shook his head in a negative manner, but he said, "Okay Natalie, give me that bow and arrow."

"I knew you'd do it," Natalie chirped. "After all, you're a hero. I expected nothing less."

As Ebol was falling through the atmosphere, he could hear Natalie calling to him, "You have one minute to string the arrow and shoot."

❧23

E bol landed behind a jeefwood on the opposite side of the clearing from where Walter sat watching Lydia and Aldersan dance. At first he was wobbly and had to lean against the tree trunk for support. Thirty precious seconds passed before he found his balance. Then, at the expense of nine more seconds, he hoisted the bow, adjusted the shaft of the arrow on the taut string, and sidled into the open.

Ebol gulped as he watched the dancers. It is a serious trial for an inexperienced archer to hit a stationary clout, and yet he was now faced with the difficult challenge of hitting a moving target.

Fifteen long seconds passed as Ebol studied the pattern of the dance. Finally he felt confident he knew where the dancers would step next. With six seconds remaining in his allotted minute, he drew back on the string. Then—just as he let the arrow fly—he was distracted by a blur of gray on the far side of the clearing.

The next thing Ebol knew he was back in heaven, watching Natalie reel with laughter.

"What happened?" he asked, but Natalie was too amused to answer. Quickly Ebol looked down, just as Aldersan Hale was leaning over to kiss Lydia Swain on the lips. Nothing funny about that, he thought. Then, at the edge of the clearing, he saw what was tickling Natalie.

It seems that the distracting gray blur at the periphery of Ebol's vision had been the mad goose, Weezie. At the exact instant that Ebol released the bow string, she had been in the act of launching a surprise attack on innocent Walter. The arrow had missed Aldersan's shoulder by inches, flown across the clearing, and struck Weezie in the tail feathers.

Poor Walter. He had no idea what was happening. Weezie had him cornered against the trunk of a jeefwood, and she was tenderly stroking his back with her long neck.

Ebol exchanged an amused glance with Natalie, then threw back his head and joined her laughing.

Evidently, Aldersan's kiss had come of its own accord.